HITTING FIFTY IN STYLE

SHORT STORY BOOK

BUSISIWE I NGWENYA

ISBN 978-0-6397-5347-8

Copy Editor: Liziwe Nkonyana

Typesetter: Zoba's Facilities

Proofreader: Busisiwe I Ngwenya

Cover Designer: Zoba's Facilities

Contact: +27 72 404 8068

Facebook: Busi Ngwenya

Twitter: @busilacoste

Email: busin@ananzi.co.za

1

CONTENTS

About the book

These short stories follow the journey of family dynamics, unexpected friendships, swindling, and ancient Egypt battles.

DEDICATION

A special thank you and gratitude to Ms Liziwe Nkonyana for spending countless hours reading and editing my work. May light keep shining on the beautiful souls who consume my work and provide feedback, much appreciated.

If only

We danced, we sang, and we loved
We debated, we fought, and we loved
We drank, we made merry, and we loved

Then fear of losing him led to control
I bullied, I obsessed, I resented
I queried, I forbade, I smothered
I spied, I eavesdropped, I crazed
How could he be so carefree
I wanted him to be all mine

Then, one day he was gone
How I miss the thunder in his voice
The passion in his face when animated
The fire in his belly when laughing
The twinkle in his when loved
I could call but pride won't allow
If only!

MADE ME BELIEVE AGAIN

"What are you doing here?" Looking up from the water tap I encountered a lanky young man eyeing me questioningly. I had been so engrossed in my thoughts that I had missed his approach and probably the gushing sound of water had also muted his footsteps.

"You should not be here…" Repeating himself as if unsure of my seemingly unresponsive conduct.

"I didn't know that drinking water from the college's tap was a crime." Getting agitated by his cryptic statements and presence when the sole intention of my being here was solitude. I needed time to digest and take in properly the scenes that were playing out at the college's assembly area.

"If I were you, I would scoot back there immediately rather than standing here and being cheeky with me." *What is wrong with this person?*

"Why?"

"I don't think you appreciate the seriousness of the situation. They are talking about you in there, and it is not looking good for you right now."

"What do you mean…" His raised hands brought home my agitation and irritation mixed with surprise at his statement whilst failing miserably to recall his name. I needed to understand how a possible strike meeting could be related to or have a bearing on me. The issues discussed there were far removed from my studies or my being at the college which is why I had taken a reprieve. Thus, the information he was sharing was strange, quite a bizarre turn of events.

"Gloria, please hurry back to the meeting right now if you know what is good for you. Oh, and please don't mention any of this to anyone."

"Okay, thanks." Taking leave of the water station I turned to walk away but stalled a bit as I needed to know. "Why do you care?"

"I have seen you around and I don't believe any of the things they are saying about you. You never seem to bother anyone."

I was surprised that he knew me that well as we have never interacted before, but I had seen him around the campus, and he had seemed like a nice guy compared to most of the 'technical' students. Moving quickly towards one of the taps upon hearing approaching footsteps, he frantically indicated with his head that I should leave. Muttering my gratitude again, I didn't need another warning and hurried back to the meeting whilst wondering why he and others got to stroll around the campus freely but yet I had to hurry back because my life might be on the line given that I had dared to leave the meeting, albeit momentarily. I joined the others just as the Amandla salutations hit frenzied proportions and reverberated through the assembly area.

Long stares and accusatory looks welcomed me back to the meeting bringing home the graveness of the matter. I was still unsure why that was happening though. Weaving and shoving I made my way through the crowd as I attempted to find an opening where I could see and hear the 'leaders' clearly. The little groupings made way whilst some nudged and nodded at each other as I edged closer to the middle of the assembly. The place was buzzing with excitement and vigour as the leaders rallied and led them in song and political slogans. There was a vulnerability and nakedness that surrounded me as I stood alone amongst united people who had seemingly found a common enemy during the period I went 'missing'.

My first encounter with political action was at the age of eight when mom and I were visiting my paternal grandparents in Soweto during the nineteen-seventy-six riots. I tasted my first teargas whilst innocently playing with a friend at my grandparents' neighbour's house who resided along the busy Baragwanath main road. We saw schoolkids marching angrily along the main road. Observed a bleeding bus driver trying to flee the scene and noticed an army casspir before we were engulfed by blinding smoke which brought immediate sore throats and a burning sensation to the eyes. Pandemonium broke as we were quickly whisked to the house before the soldiers descended on the learners with rubber bullets and more teargas. Sheer mayhem and agony that invaded my subconscious and has stayed there for years.

Thus, strikes were not new to me and nothing about this situation had gotten me excited as I could foresee its conclusion which would be in a form of toyi-toying, suspension of classes, possible college closure and missed exams. This might be followed by the leaders dumping us once their objectives were achieved or through slow erosion by spies who would report the leaders' every movement and utterances to the college's leadership. Either way, these guys would disappear and leave those of us who cannot just pack up and go in the lurch.

The saddest aspect of the unfolding events was that most of us came from poor backgrounds with parents who were barely scraping enough coins to send us to school. The impact of missing classes and exams was going to be long lasting than anyone knew or cared to admit. It was clear though that most students came from backgrounds where they had been sheltered for most of their lives and had never been exposed to strikes and state of emergency which tended to shut everything down including schooling.

Mind you, I was not opposed to some of the technical students demands which included a request for a fully equipped workshop where they could put theory into practice. This was meant to be a technical college and the balance between theory and practical work was crucial for the students as it would provide them with proper tools and skills to find work or be self-employed in the future. However, due to low numbers of technical students, it was felt important to drag the commercial side into the strike for support and to boost numbers. Some of the issues raised were new to me and I had never encountered them which ranged from racist lecturers, a rushed syllabus (they had three cycles in a year and had to learn and finish a term in three months), delayed results impacting starting time for classes and 'high' fees. They wanted the college to have a transparent scholarship programme as it was felt that the current process was not built on merit but favouritism.

Bandla, the ringleader, upon spying me in the crowd, started a frenzied speech about sell-outs and lecturers' pets who needed to be dealt with swiftly and decisively.

"We need to set an example and cut the tail of izimpimpi (spies), people who pretend to be part of the struggle whilst spying for the system. They must be taught a harsh lesson. Amandla!"

"Awethu!" The crowd responded with added oomph now that one of the 'spies' had re-joined the meeting.

"We know some of them are amongst us as we speak which is good as we need them to run to their masters and give feedback."

"Sinawe comrade, we will teach them a lesson they would never forget." Shouted a zealous follower who was frenzied up and raring to go.

"We will observe their actions before deciding on the suitable punishment." This statement was met with murmurs of disappointment and disagreement amongst the crowd but there was no one brave enough to challenge the leader openly.

"Comrades, we will be taking the memorandum with all your grievances to the Rector after this meeting. We thank you for your support and commitment to the cause, especially the commercial students." Clapping and appreciative whistling resulted in another short political song accompanied by swaying bodies and comradely leg lifts (toyi-toying).

"We will meet at the community hall at Multipurpose Centre on Monday morning to give feedback and embark on a formal strike if the discussions with the leadership don't produce the desired results today."

The concluding remarks indicated that I had missed quite a bit in the time I had been away. The meeting resolved to suspend classes for both commercial and technical students until all the students' demands were met. This being a Friday, the meeting had decided that we will be notified of the outcomes of the discussions via word-of-mouth where they would indicate whether we would return to class or go on an indefinite strike action pending the college leadership's engagement with the issues tabled.

How I envied the others freedom and ability to voice their minds, move around freely without raising an eyebrow or being judged. I still couldn't wrap my mind around the turn of events where a technical students' strike had turned into a possible full-blown college shutdown and that somehow my name, and a few others, had gotten associated with all that is evil and bad deserving of being rooted out. However, at that moment it seemed that my appearance had appeased some of the leaders somewhat and that whatever else had been raised in my absence was put to bed for now. They were currently more concerned with closing the meeting so they could go and present their demands to the leadership before the college closed for the weekend.

The proceedings were closed with the political anthem of Nkos' sikelela iAfrica before we were dismissed. Classmates and others that I had interacted with daily before that meeting avoided eye contact during the time we spent there. Taking the walk of shame towards our classroom to fetch my books felt heavy on my tiny shoulders. They failed to carry my head on this day, and it sat worryingly on my neck. Daggers and penetrative eyes pierced my back, but I willed every ounce in my body to walk naturally and almost unruffled as I didn't want to please the haters or give them something else to pin on me. I was pleased for the solitude amongst the multitudes as I needed to reflect and compose my thoughts on what lay ahead for me as a possible marked target.

"Yibo bona laba izimpimpi ezinkulu (these are the big spies)." I would recognise that voice anywhere in the college corridors or the world. It was Susan Mabunda, a classmate whom I had tried to assist with extra accounting classes, at her request, but had failed dismally as she had no aptitude for the subject, well most subjects if we were being honest. Lecturers and fellow students had tried to assist without success, but I had felt compelled to provide my services upon request. Her studies were being sponsored by her husband who wanted her to obtain a formal qualification so she could access better work opportunities. However, formal studies were proving too difficult and showed no love towards her. She battled in all lectures and the husband had threatened to de-register her as the college fees were going down the tubes.

Rumours had it that she was quite angry at my study assistance withdrawal and felt that I was solely responsible for her husband's ultimatum to de-register her. There were stories that she had mentioned that "I was not all that" or "that I thought I was better" and it seemed that she had been waiting for the day where I could be nailed to the must for being "snooty and mighty". These comments made me wonder at her involvement in my being fingered as a possible spy given the limited interaction between the technical and commercial students. Based on the direction of my thoughts and the bitterness that visited my heart I realised that it was best I went home to mama for parental soothing and guidance before a terrible confrontation ensued.

Lazarus Nhlapho Technical College had not been my first choice; however, it had presented that façade of a possible escape from parental control to adulthood and freedom after high school completion. My parents, particularly my mom, were big on education and it didn't matter which route you took as long as it came in a form of a formal education setting. I was a very creative individual but that was not deemed a stable career and the college route was imposed on me by my dad when my six months sojourn with a fly-by-night drama school fizzled into a shattered dream and lost funds for the parents.

The college was split into commercial and technical studies with conflicting study schedules where both streams attended classes at different intervals except during the first and last semester. We didn't mingle much with the technical students as most of them tended to look down upon commercial students, especially those of us who were focusing on secretarial studies. These were seen as girly, easy and not worth much, they probably thought we lacked intelligence and drive. This made us avoid them at all costs as they showed patriarchy and arrogance towards us. Thus, when rumours of their alleged dissatisfaction with the Rector and certain lecturers surfaced, we didn't pay much attention to them initially as the grievances affected "the snobs" of the college.

They quickly learnt that they carried little muscle as most technical students were done with their studies for that term and some were studying part-time. Thus, they somehow managed to worm their way towards a few 'weak' ones or people with own agendas amongst the commerce students. These talks had been strengthened when both camps found commonalities regarding favouritism, 'unqualified' lecturers, and inferior lecturing. There were rumours that some of the lecturers had never gone beyond tenth grade and that only a handful had bachelor's degrees whilst the rest boasted some technical skill or a matriculation certificate with a secretarial or artisan certificate here and there.

Susan and I had joined the college in the same year doing secretarial studies and were in a class of eight students. I made firm friends with Ziphora and was partial to Joyce's warm, boisterous, and outgoing personality. Susan, Ziphora, and I travelled together after class as we stayed in the same vicinity and lived a few blocks apart. Relations with Susan were cordial and platonic initially moving to cold when I dropped her as 'my learner'. Unbeknown to me the severed tutor/student relation cut so deep that she was willing to spread false rumours when Bandla and the student leaders were looking for culprits they could nail as sell-outs. This type of hatred cut deep as it was common for comrades to put a tyre on 'spies' and burn them alive as a warning to others. It was scary that a classmate would go to those lengths to vent her dissatisfaction by daring to put someone's life in danger in that fashion. It felt as if there might have been more at play than the tutoring withdrawal. I was not her lecturer after all, this had been done as a favour at no cost to her.

Weeping and self-pity were not entertained in the Ndimande household, but the parents helped explore the position I found myself in. We resolved that I was going to attend all the meetings when word reached us that the negotiations had failed, and we were in full strike mode. We were grateful that these meetings were to be held in a place within walking distance from home, bringing a huge saving on transport and lunch money.

Monday found me at the meeting place at the appointed time and there were a few shocked faces at my attendance which I ignored. There was a feeling of rejection and distrust towards me which brought fear as I became unsure about my safety until one of the leaders came over and expressed his appreciation for my support and attendance. We found a sitting spot and chatted away until the meeting resumed after signing-in. Susan and others were in attendance and avoided me like a plague. That student leader became a firm friend and my salvation in my bleakest hour and restored my faith in humans. The strike lasted over two months and most people dropped from college along the way and it was sad when I lost my buddy as well.

"Dude, this is my last meeting." He stated sadly during a cold rainy day.

"What do you mean? The strike is not over yet."

"I travel daily from Soweto to Tembisa to just sit and attend fruitless meetings. My parents have been supportive, but the prolonged strike has seen them withdraw financial support. The attendance is getting costly."

"Oh—"

"You will be fine. The leadership trusts you now and know that those rumours were false and malicious intended to tarnish your name and bring harm to you."

"Oh—" Words deserted my vocabulary, but it seemed that they were not necessary.

"Some people had it in for you and we were also unsure of you when you showed up for the first meeting. Yet, you looked so vulnerable and gave me the urge to wanna protect you, I am glad you proved me right." *Wow, so I was under scrutiny for the most part.*

"Your continued support and attendance saved your life. They were gunning for you and a few others, some of whom were dealt with."

Well, there you have it. I was out of the woods and safe now, but the victory felt hollow as I was losing a good friend and confidant. My gut told me that our paths will never cross after this episode.

"Thank you for everything."

"It is a pleasure dude. Do take care." Saying goodbye was sad and even sadder was the strike losing its oomph two weeks later. Many other students fell along the way including Bandla, Susan, Joyce, and Ziphora.

We went back to college and knuckled down to finish our studies, but the carefree student life was gone. College life was never the same without some of the kids who were forced to drop out due to financial difficulties and/or discouragement or fatigue. I survived possible necklacing (term coined for the tyre around your neck system) because of entitled and malicious beings, but in the process I obtained a true friend and protector from the most unexpected source who made me believe again in humanity. I made it my mission to be better and more focused for him and others who had dared to dream but lost the fight along the way.

ATONEMENT

Luke was becoming agitated with how long it was taking the guys to secure the last target. In this business timing was of essence and keeping to the plan was a must. He was concerned that the two girls lying on the back seat might start weaning off the drugs and cause a scene. He didn't want trouble or to deal with hysterical females. That was not part of his job description. He was a driver and it all ended there. Everyone, including his boss knew about this. He didn't compromise or engage himself in matters that were not part of his mandate except in extraordinary cases that were of death and survival.

He checked his watch for the umpteenth time and realised that the cloak's hands had barely moved since he had last looked at it thirty seconds ago. He was also in dire need of a puff, but cigarettes were discouraged in this business. In fact, any traceable conduct was not allowed especially things that could easily be avoided like cigarette butts. It was surprising how unsympathetic non-smokers were to people like him but would fidget and demand attention when tables were turned, and they couldn't access liquor or water or food. *Quite selfish individuals if you ask me.*

Luke sighed with relief when he spotted his accomplices (Vic and Mo) strolling gently with the last girl heading towards his direction through the open parking lot of Woodmead shopping complex. Anyone looking at them would have assumed that the young lady had consumed copious amount of alcohol and her caring friends were ensuring that she reached the sanctuary of the car without tripping. Vic had his arms around the victim's waist in what seemed like a lover's embrace to a naked eye with Mo carrying her handbag as they made their way to the car. He found this showy conduct troubling and saw a few on-lookers throwing curious looks towards them prompting him to spring into action and meet them halfway.

"There was no need for that brother." Vic commented with a puzzled look once seated.

"You were taking too long and drawing attention to yourselves." Luke replied calmly as he navigated the car out of Woodmead and headed towards the M1. He couldn't wait to dump the guys and the passengers so he could head out to Braamfontein for some grown-up company and relaxation at Leano Restaurant and Live Music place.

"You know we have to act casual so as to not raise unnecessary attention." Mo stated.

Luke grunted as he joined the N1 leading towards the drop off.

"No worries." Luke felt compelled to calm them down, resulting in him momentarily taking his eyes off the road.

"Hey watch out! Some of us have families to feed. One would swear you have never done this job before." Vic shouted.

"Sorry." Luke tossed the apology as he narrowly avoided hitting a police van which would have been a disaster given their cargo. He raised an apologetic hand at the cops as he didn't fancy an altercation with the blue brigade, even though some of them could easily be bought off with as little as fifty rands.

He turned briefly to take a proper look at the new girl sprawled at the seat behind him and almost lost his footing. The last young woman was an exact replica of Sihle, his teen daughter who was abducted twenty years ago and whose mutilated corpse was recovered on their street corner dumpster a couple of days later by waste management crew. Quite a gruesome death that was. It was probably more shocking that someone like him would end up in this line of work but that is the sad outcome of tragedy because it can either turn you into a Mother Teresa or a bleeding monster. This girl had the same East African exotic looks, fine limbs, and perfect glowing skin like his Sihle. The resemblance was uncanny, and he knew that he couldn't live with himself if he didn't attempt to set her free. It would be a befitting homage to his deceased daughter whom he couldn't save.

"You don't seem well brother. Please pull over so I can take over. We cannot afford to cause or get into an accident." Luke gladly stopped the car and allowed Vic to take the wheel as he felt that he would be in a better position to think properly. He never involved himself with the abductions and always disappeared after making a drop off but this time it was different. He felt compelled to assist the girl and had to devise ways to befriend her between tonight and tomorrow evening before the handover. It was not going to be easy though given their drug-induced state.

"You don't seem well."

"Lost a bundle at the casino. The madam is not happy."

"I have warned about that."

"I know."

"You should have stayed at home."

"No, I needed this. I would like to travel with the handover crew."

"Why? You never take part in these things and have never shown any interest before."

"I need a break from Jozi, and this trip would do me good. Besides I need the money."

"Well, we do need extra hands. We are currently short-staffed. There is a huge demand from Europe for our girls and we cannot keep up. The sooner we can get them moving the better."

"Cool, I will leave the coordination in your capable hands Vic." He stated casually whilst pulling back the seat recliner to lounge nonchalantly as if unconcerned about the outcome.

Vic pondered the matter further and shrugged slightly indicating that this matter was not really under his control. They finished the last few minutes of the journey in a comfortable silence as each mulled over the events leading to this moment.

They pulled into one of those plush and leafy suburbs surrounded by tall brick walls, electric fencing, and huge trees. Places where the rich and famous played and didn't care much about neighbours' as long as they didn't cause mayhem or disturbance to the community. Vic punched in numbers on the hidden keypad and the gate opened to reveal what looked like a palace in Luke's eyes. I could get used to this life, he thought. *These girls are definitely special.*

"Hmmm classy hey Vic. Not the usual hangout."

"Last minute changes to the plan due to some high-profile girl disappearing this afternoon."

Vic informed him that the transportation of the girls was delayed by a few days due to heightened public outcry over the missing girl, much to Luke's surprise

27

and delight. News coming in was that a high-profile kid had been snatched a few hours earlier on her way home from watching movies with friends. The driver had stopped at a convenient store as the girl had wanted to buy snacks. She had been snatched in front of the store as she stepped out. The incident had happened so suddenly that it had taken the driver and staff of the convenience store by surprise resulting in a couple of minutes delay before cops were called and a chase ensued. The girl had not been recovered as yet and the police were on high alert for a red VW Passat (probably long abandoned).

Luke shook his head in anger and wonder that no one had thought it prudent to pull a plug on their assignment given the circumstances. He was also unimpressed with himself for not being a news junkie as he would have known about the incident and been on higher alert. He was grateful that everything had gone accordingly thus far and that the girls were staying for a while.

It seemed that he was the only one left behind, not surprising though given that he was just a mere getaway driver and did not get involved in the physical abductions of the girls but still...

"We are going to lay low here for a couple of days until we get the greenlight to move the girls. We will be responsible for keeping them safe, clean, fed and sedated as we don't need unnecessary attention from neighbours."

They got out of the car and carried each girl inside as they were still comatose. They put the girls in separate bedrooms with their ankles and wrists bound and their mouths gagged to ensure that they did not cause a racket when they recovered. Luke offered to check on the girls every four hours to ensure that they were physically fine and fed which Vic appreciated before adding sarcastically.

"Don't get too attached. They will be gone before you know it."

He woke up early to prepare breakfast and arranged with Vic to bring one of their ladies to assist the girls with bathing issues. Martha, who had no motherly instinct or any warmth in any body part, was brought in. Her whole demeanour was that of an army sergeant which didn't encourage backchatting or misconduct; she was tough. Luke and Martha took turns to feed the girls and ensured that they were comfortable. He rotated between the girls so as not to raise suspicion in his quest to discover more about the girl.

She looked confused and scared the first time she laid eyes on him and kept asking for her mom. "Momma must be worried, and her heart would not hold for long if I don't return home soon." She implored Luke on their first face-to-face meeting.

"Out of my hands baby girl, sorry. Who is your mom if I may ask?"

"Why?" Fear and anxiety filled that one word as the reality of her situation sunk in.

"Nothing. Just making a conversation. Eat your food."

"Her name is Zodwani…" The girl stopped unnerved by his reaction.

Luke shifted uncomfortably. Surely, it can't be. They only had one child. He was sure of that but then again, he had disappeared soon after the funeral never to be seen. No contact whatsoever. He could not face her. He had failed to protect their precious angel from evil. He had left Zodwani to deal with the loss alone whilst he numbed himself with booze and drugs until a mere chance with his current boss who had been almost cornered by would be hijackers. Luke had been alert enough to jump in and push his way through in an attempt to save the man, for reasons unknown to him.

He had shoved the guy to the passenger seat and driven off the scene like a maniac. Years of working as a mechanic who test drove people's cars and did weekend spins at Khayalami re-surfacing. The man was so impressed with his driving skills that he had been hired on the spot with no questions asked except an order to sober-up. No, it must be a coincidence. Surely, there were other Zodwani's out there even though hers was an uncommon name.

They sat in uncomfortable silence as she nibbled on her food whilst he mulled on the issue.

"What were you doing at the club all by yourself in this country known for its disregard for women, especially pretty girls like you?" Luke ventured on the third day when visiting her again.

"My supposed friend invited me to her birthday party. I think it was a set-up because no-one showed up and the venue had no booking under her name." Sighing heavily as she realised again the danger she had been put in and was unsure why she was confiding in one of the crooks. She had sat at the bar and ordered a cola whilst attempting to reach her friend. At some point she had attempted to leave as her body got heavy, but her limbs had refused to move, resulting in the waiter summoning the two men to help her out.

Luke felt sorry for the girl for being duped in this manner. He renewed his vow to do everything in his power to set her free whatever the cost to his own life, especially given that she could be from his semen.

The friendship between Luke and the girl grew as the days stretched into a week with no indication of the handover date. Then out of the blue Vic burst into the house to announce their departure that night.

"Brothers, word finally came in. We are transporting the cargo tonight for Namibia where it will catch a flight to Amsterdam. Our border immigration person has sorted out all the paperwork and we will take turns driving through the night for Namibia." Vic paused to see if Luke and Mo had any questions and proceeded when none were forthcoming. "Our middleman is getting anxious as money was exchanged and the clients are getting impatient to receive their cargo."

Luke, Mo, and Vic pored over the logistics of transporting the girls from South Africa and the handover to their Namibian counterparts who will travel with the girls from Windhoek to Amsterdam. Luke avoided visiting the girl that day and left everything to Martha as he finalised her getaway plans.

Martha administered enough drugs into the girls' system to keep them numb but awake. They carried them to the back of the panel van and Luke used that opportunity to slip an airtag into the girl's pocket. He had engineered the whole thing in such a way that he was responsible for bolting the van's doors and could slip the devise unobserved.

He drove moderately as they left Gauteng for Namibia via Kuruman as they didn't want to deal with the Botswana border. He increased the speed considerably as they approached Ventersdorp leading Vic to raise a concern.

"Bro, are you on drugs or something?"

"No, why?"

"You drove like a donkey for the past two hours and now this?"

"Sorry, my bad."

"We need to get the girls alive at the border." A calmer Vic stated.

"Sure."

They passed an idle truck outside Ventersdorp which suddenly joined the road and charged after them at an alarming speed, leading Luke to driver even faster.

"What the hell?" Vic shouted as he cocked his gun ready to shoot at the menace behind them. Just then an on-coming tow truck (appearing from the bushes) joined the road from the opposite direction and unexpectedly swerved into their lane forcing Luke to duck violently.

"Watch out!" Vic shouted as Luke narrowly avoided a collision only to be rammed on the side by the truck resulting in him letting go of the van which rolled a couple of times before lending on its roof. Running footsteps approached the van, the girls were offloaded, and whisked away. Luke heaved a relieved breath knowing that the girls were safe as he lay there preparing himself for the consequences. His plan had worked. Hopefully, they might not be able to pin this on him but if they did, he would rest in peace knowing that he had saved his girl this time around. He hoped that Zodwani would know and forgive him for deserting her years ago when she had needed him the most. This act would serve as atonement, hopefully.

HITTING FIFTY IN STYLE

Sonto sat on the swing of her front porch reminiscing over her youthful days as she paged through her collection of photo albums to revive her spirits over singledom. She mused over the pictures taken during family vacations, which generally, comprised of visits to aunts or uncles in far off places like eNquthu, Dundee, Pietermaritzburg, or Mount Frere. The visits were never planned but depended on the availability of funds and which relative was willing to accommodate the Pastor's kids over the festivities. Most took them in out of pity as they understood that paid-up holidays were out of the family's reach and others, like aunt Snothie, were more excited about digging in the 'Christmas' box goodies the kids brought along. The box was an annual bonus package received from her mom's employers.

There she was in her afro, black and pink polka dots midi-dress, big loop earrings with white platform shoes completing the look. These were in fashion and quite popular in the 80s making her part of the 'it' group. She was a fashionista of note and bought whatever she wanted with money made selling lollipops and braiding hair which was all hers. Most of it went towards her allowance and school uniform, she was a buccaneer shoes girl and would not compromise on this. Her parents only had to pay school fees and buy the required stationery. Boys were attracted to her like bees to nectar and could never seem to get enough of her caramel complexion, big eyes, rounded face, flat stomach, and long legs. She belonged in cover magazines, if only her parents could have seen that and utilised that potential to make money and live comfortably as the family deserved. Nonetheless, she had used her beauty and brain to lure customers and made money for her businesses. In her school and university days she never lacked money or the attention of men, until she reached her late forties.

She still had money, beauty, and brains but men had dissipated. The only male attention she seemed to attract these days was that of security men asking about her health, her pastor checking why she has not been to church or her gardener asking for new equipment or a day off. On occasion there would be that odd truck driver hooting his acknowledgement at her swaying hips and shapely legs but that is where it ended. How she longed for a companion, someone she could share her lifestyle and grow old with. As the years rolled by this dream seemed to be getting further and further away and she was afraid that after fifty it would be unattainable rendering her a spinster like her aunt Mavis who had become a family joke and matter of ridicule for her childless and 'man less' life. Initially, this did not matter to her at all as she chased after her dreams and kept on climbing the corporate ladder until that fateful day when she had collapsed from mental exhaustion and burnout.

The last three years were spent nursing herself back to health and building her empire in the advertising space. It had been a slow and painful journey where there were more days to a month during certain periods, but she had persevered. Now she was starting to reap the benefits of all that hard work and all that was missing was that special someone to share her life with. She had lost her only daughter, Lindo, to a car incident with her behind the wheel.

They were returning from grocery shopping and cruising along Ben Schoeman Highway when the truck in front of them lost its load (it was carrying pallets). She had managed to swerve out of danger but lost control due to oversteering and ended up hitting an electricity pole which fell on top of the passenger side killing her precious princess instantly. It took years to recover from that tragedy and she had buried most of the hurt and guilt in her work. The emotional toil and stress had finally caught up with her three years ago. She had learnt a valuable lesson from that journey, which is that you cannot bury or run away from pain. It will manifest itself in your body through various, mostly unseen ways, until the day it decided to release itself in a form of cancer, brain tumour, kidneys, or stroke.

One thing Sonto wanted to avoid at all costs, was to celebrate her half century milestone alone and she was determined to explore all options at her disposal to find that companion. So far, she had tried church, as per recommendation from a friend, but found the noise too much to handle. It had felt like being at a rock concert and that was no longer her vibe. She had then tried shopping at Checkers and Woolworths in places like the Mall of Africa, Sandton City, and Brooklyn Mall as per Steve Harvey's recommendation that good men can be found at grocery stores. All she found were hurried and harassed women and/or families and nothing resembling a fine male specimen she could attach herself to (he was probably talking about the US grocery stores).

She had never been sold on blind dates or online dating and was even more scared of those after the Tinder Swindler story, which limited her choices of finding a man even more. Breakfast and brunch runs were fun but tended to be crowded by cyclists who moved in crowds, and she was never sure whether it would be appropriate to approach a potential man in that set-up. Running or any sporting events just did not grab her attention. She suspected that those people went there to distress and not look for dates because who would in their minds wake up very early in the morning to go pound the tar without any provocation, this never made sense to her.

The ringing of her landline, yes, she still had one of those as she could be weird like that, cut through her musings and she was startled that she had spent the better part of her morning reminiscing. She lifted her legs off the coffee table, put on her pink fluffy sleepers with dog ears, tribute to her daughter who had loved animals, and made her way leisurely to the lounge. She was not bothered by the phone cutting, as her philosophy was that people would hang on a bit more or leave a message if they were desperate to chat.

"Sonto speaking, hello?"

"That took long enough, were you sleeping?" Trust Dora to be abrupt and not greet.

"Morning my dear friend."

"Stop the nonsense, what took you so long? Anyway, never mind. A group of women at work have organised a cruise trip to the Cayman Islands and am tempted to join them if only I could get you to come with…"

"You tried everybody, and they said no right? Which is why you are calling?" Sonto knew Dora very well. Dora considered her a bit mild and a party pooper at most times much as there was love between them. She must be quite desperate to invite her on this trip.

"Yah well, I am not going to lie. People have commitments or financial challenges, and you are the only person I know who is flexible enough to do this. Besides, Cayman Islands are on your bucket list. Let's do this before you turn fifty and who knows your Mr. Right might be on that cruise or at the Islands. Hmm---"

Sonto did not want to lie, the proposal including the costs was quite tempting and the dates were doable which made it impossible to say no. Cayman Islands were indeed on her must visit list. Although, on her wish list the Islands always featured a male companion by her side, not Dora and her colleagues. Ahh well, this might be what she needed to get herself out of the rut and she might get her groove back on like Stella. She found herself nodding enthusiastically forgetting that she was on the phone and was brought back to the present when Dora asked for her response.

"Yes, count me in and send the itinerary with all the logistics and final budget please." Sonto concluded before bidding her friend farewell and bouncing off to her bedroom to prepare for the day. She had a few meetings lined up in the afternoon and she needed to catch up with her personal assistant so they can re-arrange her calendar to fit in the trip. This was going to be great; she could feel it. Cayman Islands here we come, she shouted triumphantly and happily as she made her way to the office with a newfound spring in her step.

They were going to fly from OR Tambo International Airport to George Town in the Bahamas via Doha and catch a ferry from there to the Islands. Sonto spent most of the remaining days before the trip finalising important work at the office, getting travel clothing and sorting out related logistics. They were spending a night at George Town before transferring to Cayman Islands where they were booked to stay a week at the Luxury Cayman Villas located in Seven Mile Beach, the place looked quite lovely based on the pictures which of course can be deceiving but she was optimistic that it would deliver.

The trip was quite uneventful, except the hours spent travelling, and before she knew it, they were at the Islands. They were booked at the Kaia Kamina which had seven bedrooms, making it possible for the group of fourteen ladies to be in the same Villa, which was opulent and elegant, and was right on the beach with breathtakingly stunning views, with a pool leading directly to the white sandy beach with clear blue water. The rooms were bright and airy, and Sonto did not mind sharing a bedroom with Dora as they had been friends since primary school and had been there for each other through thick and thin.

The ladies had a packed itinerary consisting of kayaking, boat rides, snorkelling, clubbing, and a full day Islands tour. She intended doing everything on offer but reserved a Wednesday to herself for spa treatments and relaxation. On Wednesday she was

43

shuttled to the InSPAration Cayman spa as arranged and was pleasantly happy with the set-up which had sea facing massage rooms and you could even choose to be massaged outside as close to the beach as possible. There was a gentleman at the reception counter as she stepped in, and she waited patiently as they finalised his booking.

"Thank you, Sir, your therapist will take you through. Do enjoy our service." Sonto was fascinated by the stature of the man, he held himself with dignity and assurance of someone used to being served. The greyish hair was cut quite short and made his pixie ears stand out sharply. Nice body shape encased in grey chinos, white t-shirt and khakhi loafers giving a relaxed holiday look. Sonto was fascinated by the rear and could not wait for him to turn around so she could see if the promised package delivered fully.

"Next—" Sonto realised from the raised tones that she had been so lost in her scrutiny of the gentleman that she had lost track of her surroundings. She moved quickly forward with burning cheeks and slightly downcast eyes as everyone had turned to look at her, including the object of her scrutiny. Ooh my, did he deliver! It was yumminess of olive dark skin, brown eyes and a face which could not be described as handsome but more likely as dreamy or unforgettable. He was an attractive gentleman, possibly a few years ahead of her, who oozed physical and sensuality promises. She shivered with yearning as she brushed past him to reach the reception desk.

"Morning Ma'am. How can we help?"

"Morning, I am Sonto. I have a ten AM spa treatment appointment." She was grateful that years of communication and public speaking trainings were her saving grace as they helped disguise the tremors she felt inside.

"Oh, yes Ma'am. Everything is in order. I am your therapist. Please complete this form for me and let me know when done." Sonto completed all the administration requirements and was taken through to her massage room, she was slightly disappointed to have not had the opportunity to admire the gentleman again.

She was done with her treatments three hours later and was grateful to be offered sweet tea and some nibbles before leaving as she felt quite famished. They directed her to the terrace to enjoy the view whilst sipping on her tea and was pleasantly surprised when the gentleman she had seen earlier came out and asked to join her.

"I was getting worried that you might be in there for the whole day." What an introduction thought Sonto.

"I was booked for three treatments but why would that be of concern to you, if I may ask?"

"Because I am famished, and I would like to share my lunch with you." *Quite forward hey, does he think I am an easy pick?*

"I am sorry you had to wait that long for nothing…"

"What do you mean?" Ah, arrogance gone now.

"I am having lunch with my friends. They are not into massages; hence I came alone. In fact, I should be leaving."

"Oh, what a pity. Dinner then? I promise I won't bite, and I can be quite a gentleman when dealing with a fine young lady like you." Gosh, what a flatterer and charmer.

The receptionist came out then to inform her that her transportation had arrived. She took the extended business card with his name on it and added before leaving.

"My name is Sonto. See you around Allan."

Sonto never saw Allan again until they left the Islands and wondered whether she should have given her contacts or called him to arrange a meeting but had been hesitant as she had not wanted to appear too forward or needy. Life returned to normal once she reached home. She buried herself in office work having concluded that dating at her age was gonna be an uphill battle. As her fiftieth birthday loomed closer and larger than a heavy storm, she wondered whether it was worth throwing a big party where most of her family and childhood friends will pitch with their spouses or partners to celebrate her lonesomeness. She was even tempted to reconcile with Lindo's dad but quickly recoiled from the idea as flashes of their life together re-surfaced.

He was a good man and had taken care of their daughter's needs until her passing. He was a loner and never destined to be around or surrounded by people. He did not do well in public spaces and was always searching for work opportunities that required working in isolation or being on the road for extended periods. Sonto had initially enjoyed the freedom it brought but later realised that she needed the companionship, warmth, romance, and lovemaking more than the extended lonely spells, so had ended the relationship as she went in search of permanency which had eluded her so far.

She noted missed calls from the event organiser and knew that she was getting frustrated at her lack of commitment as the day of the celebrations got closer. She wondered what it was that held her back from cancelling, must be wishful thinking or fear of disappointing people when they were all geared up for what was termed as "the mothership of all parties". Outfits had been sourced, venue secured, band booked, pastor scheduled, flower arrangement and cake organised including a DJ and speakers. There was no going back now, she thought as she picked up her phone to return the calls but was interrupted by an incoming call.

"You play hard to get hey!" What was that? Sonto stared at the phone in shock before responding.

"Who is this?" She demanded.

"You know my dear only men behave in this manner…"

"Look I don't have time to play. Who are you and what do you want?" A heavy sigh filled with impatience filled the telephone line making Sonto reach for the end call button but wait a minute…that voice.

"Allan, is that you?"

"Ahh, she remembers my name. Progress indeed." Mxm, what is it with this man.

"How can I help you?"

"Oh, my dear, am still waiting to take you out for lunch or dinner. You never called so I decided to make a fool of myself again. I am hoping that this time you will agree." Sonto was lost, how did he find her? Yet here he was acting like they last saw each other yesterday. Such arrogance was incomprehensible to be honest.

"It can't be such a tough decision, especially for someone who runs a successful enterprise as yourself. Are you joining me for lunch or not?"

"How, when you are based in the Bahamas?"

"Oh, these things can be arranged. So, are you finally accepting my invite?"

"Yes, I would love to go out with you." What do I have to lose? Besides, we will meet in my turf so I will have a home advantage.

"Great, I will make travel arrangements and you can pick me up at the airport so we can go somewhere close by as I would need to fly out afterwards." What! The man was crazy, who flies all the way from the Bahamas to come eat and fly out again. Madness, I tell you.

"I have a better proposal for you. I will be turning fifty in the next few months and am throwing a party to celebrate this milestone. Why don't you come through for the festivities and join me as my special guest for the night? Anyway, I need a date."

"No, my dear. I am a stranger to you and your friends, it is proper that we meet first and get to know each other before we go that route, please."

A deflated but understanding Sonto agreed on the proposed day for their first date. She managed to convince Allan to spend a night in the country to soak in its beauty and get acclimatised with the environment as there was a chance that there might be more dates in the future.

She knocked off early on the day Allan was landing and headed to the salon to have her braids washed and styled. She also did her nails and make-up before heading to the shops to find an outfit for the date before driving off to OR Tambo International Airport at the appointed time to pick up Allan. He strode off the arrival gates on time as he had no baggage to clear except an overnight bag with few essentials and a laptop. He hugged and kissed her ferociously, literally devouring her like a hungry man who had not snacked on a human body in a long time. Sonto was a bit squirmish at first but soon found herself consumed by the same fire which had taken over Allan. It was only when she surfaced from the embrace to inhale some air that she caught site of a traffic cop approaching that her senses returned, and she made a quick getaway before landing an unwanted ticket.

"Whew, that was beautiful like you my dear lady. Hello Sonto." Startled she turned around to look at him properly before returning her eyes to the road again.

"What, you thought I couldn't pronounce your name?"

"Yeah, the thought did cross my mind. Who taught you that?" Realising how melodic and unexpected the sound of her name coming from his lips had been. She hoped that there would be more of those based on that airport kiss which was mind blowing. It had brought moistness accompanied with lust having spent years without any sexual activity, the longing was huge.

"I can do many things when inspired. How are you feeling my dear and where are you taking me?"

"I made a booking at Fairlawns Boutique Hotel as they are not too far off from the airport and do provide food and accommodation. I thought you would be tired from the long trip and didn't want you moving around a lot. We can sit in your room or in the gardens and catch up before dinner."

"Sitting in the garden would be lovely. I have been in airplanes for too long. I am going to take a nap if you don't mind dear."

"No stress, I will wake you up when we get there." Sonto agreed, although slightly disappointed as she had wanted to converse as much as possible, but this was not bad either as she had ample time to stare and just take him in.

"You are staring." Ugh how did he know? Sonto felt slightly embarrassed but then decided that she was not going to deprive herself of such a rare opportunity and thus continued to stare whenever she could. The ride to the hotel was uneventful and in twenty minutes they were off ramping to take the M60, join M74 and then M85 which would take them to the hotel.

Allan checked in, requested Sonto to sort out their dinner whilst he took a refreshing shower. She was slightly disappointed as she had thought that they would spend time together in the room but said nothing as she did not want to look desperate or too forward. Dinner was lovely, and the company was great with lots of banter and laughter between them. They spent a great evening getting to know each other and Allan sent Sonto on her way around ten PM as he "wanted her home safe before it got too late given the crime in the country."

They spent the following day shopping at Sandton City and later explored Maropeng Cradle of Humankind before heading to the airport for Allan's late-night flight. Sonto was happy with time spent with Allan and looked forward to their next meeting which was planned for the next month where Allan intended to spend three or four days with her.

The parting was quite emotional and sad with the only consolation being that they were now a couple and will be able to keep in constant contact. Allan reported the following evening that he had travelled well and was back at work. He thanked Sonto for her hospitality and time showing him around some main attractions in Gauteng.

Allan made a strange call a week before his third visit to the country which amazed and excited Sonto. He stated that he was thinking of moving his business interests to the South. Possibly moving in with her until they found a place most suitable to them and their needs, stating that he would take care of everything. Sonto was not averse to the idea having mulled over it and affirming that long distance relationships did not work well for her. It was agreed that Allan would first move in on a trial basis to assess whether they were compatible living together and if Mzansi suited him. He would later go back home to take stock and wrap outstanding business matters, if he decided to move permanently, sort out business permit issues before his final return.

Sonto and Allan spent most of this visit going to the different government departments and agencies like Home Affairs, CIPC, SARS and others to gain knowledge on trading requirements for foreigners. Allan requested Sonto to initiate the house hunting process whilst he was gone and line up viewings upon his return on at least three of her top five homes. The budget was set at five million rands as Allan indicated that money would be coming from the sale of his home and some business interests.

Sonto roped in Dora in her house search but was quite not sold on the idea as she loved her house and the area that she lived in. She had spent a considerable amount and time designing it to her taste and requirements and did not think she would find something quite like it. However, she attempted to find something within the price bracket provided and most of the places were either in estates or complexes which was not ideal for her. She liked and preferred to be as far as possible from her neighbours giving her the privacy required away from constant prying eyes.

"Hello, Sonto my love." Allan's calls were filling her with anxiety lately as she had not committed to any place yet and he was due in the country in the next two weeks.

"Hello, love. How are things?" Sonto asked trying to infuse some excitement.

"Everything is wrapped up and shipment of my goods has been finalised. They should be there three weeks after my arrival."

"That's wonderful news dear."

"Have you found a place yet?"

"We went out again this weekend and most places I liked are either too far out or above our budget. There are a few that we can view though when you arrive."

"That's great. I have managed to raise fifty thousand dollars…"

"Which would give us seven hundred and sixty-four thousand rands as things stand which is nowhere near what we are looking at in terms of our house search."

Misgivings clouded Sonto's mind before she dismissed them quickly as she did not want to engage in negative thoughts whilst planning a bright future with her man.

"You worry too much Sonto. The money will come through once all the legalities and transfers have taken place."

"Yes, love. See you soon."

"Yeah, I can't wait. Take care, lots of love." Allan signed off with his signature blowing of kisses over the phone line routine.

He wired the money as promised which was to go towards the house deposit and Sonto let it sit in her bank account waiting for it to clear but also determined that she would finalise the buying of the house with him present. The big day finally arrived, weeks before her fiftieth, where she had to pick him up from the airport for the last time as a visitor. She decided to throw a welcome party and invited a few family members and friends who knew of or had met Allan by now. The festivities went on until the early hours of the morning and it was only when Sonto noticed the fatigue on Allan's face that she called it a day, having remembered the hours he had travelled.

She had been so busy lately with financial year-end preparations at work and upcoming birthday party co-ordination that it took her a while to notice that house hunting had stalled to the ground and that Allan seemed to spend more and more time indoors than sorting out business issues. She resolved to raise the matter once she became aware of it. She also noticed that groceries were running faster than a Ferrari, especially the tomato sauce which the man was smearing on everything. She had been taken aback when she caught him putting a large dollop of tomato sauce on an apple. To make matters, he was not contributing anything towards his upkeep since he landed. Something was just not adding up.

The large sum of money that he had deposited whilst still in the Bahamas had not cleared yet and just sat there unable to be used. This did not seem to bother Allan as he kept assuring her that legalities took time in his home country but insisted that everything will work out, things were not making sense.

One day Sonto arrived to an empty house with no sign of Allan and there was no message on her phone or note on the table as was the norm when he had to go out unexpectedly and did not want to trouble her. She dialled his number, but the phone went to voicemail. She gave up on the third attempt and rather made an impromptu coffee date with Dora as she needed an objective person to lend an ear to her troubled thoughts.

Mugg & Bean lemonade juice had her name written all over it, she could already envision it as she walked through their doors with Dora following closely behind.

"Hi, we want to sit at that far corner table please." The waitress nodded and led them to their table.

"Thank you sisi, I don't know about my friend, but I know what I want. May I please have your bottomless lemonade juice and toasted chicken mayo sandwich with potato fries."

Poor Dora found herself scrambling and paging through the menu trying to decide on what she wanted to have just keep up with Sonto.

"Don't rush Ma'am. I will come back for your order." Dora sighed gratefully and settled back on her chair to view the menu at leisure. She focused questioning eyes on Sonto once satisfied with her food choice.

"What's happening, talk to me?"

"I have just realised that I don't know much about Allan, and I invited him to my home and country without even investigating him which is so unlike me."

"Yes, you fell quickly and behaved like an adolescent which is okay when you are just having fun but not when you go all in. He seems to love you though---" Dora's hanging sentence brought back the anxieties Sonto had been having lately.

"I think he does, my issue is that for a businessperson he does not seem invested in anything."

"Yes, I would have expected him to hit the ground running sorting out his business and financial issues. What does he say?"

"I went home early to raise these issues with him only to find an empty house with no messages of his whereabout."

"Strange, you need to have a serious chat with him." Sonto paused as the waitress brought her drink and took Dora's order.

"That was my intention today. I have been so focused on the year-end activities that I lost track of my personal life."

"You know I am always there for you no matter what happens."

"I do and I appreciate you very much my friend, cheers to a meaningful and joyful life."

Sonto wondered why she could never find a down-to-earth and no-frills guy like Dora's husband. Always tinkering in the garage or garden if not at the construction site. Never had time for ladies, in fact guys used to laugh at him growing up for 'igwababa' and were amazed when he managed to catch a strong personality like Dora, a case of polar opposites attracting.

"Sonto your phone is ringing."

"Oh, thanks. It's him. Hello love."

Dora observed Sonto's face but could not decipher from her poker face whether Allan was alright or not. She shrugged and focused on her cappuccino whilst itching for the one-sided call to end so they could catch up.

"You won't believe this. Allan said he was at the construction site in our area." Sonto stated with confusion.

"Looking for a house?"

"No, working. He says he managed to find contract work there which will assist to bring in some needed cash whilst he waits for his things to clear."

"What, I am confused." Dora slowly put her cup down and stared at Sonto, confusion and curiosity plastered all over her concerned face.

"It is quite clear my friend. There is no money coming through and that man does not own any businesses which is why that deposit has not cleared…"

"Whoa whoa my friend. You are jumping to a conclusion. Write down your concerns and have a discussion with him around those before you make assumptions."

Sonto just shrugged unconvinced as she realised that an investigation was required before she resolved on the way forward with Allan, something she should have done before he moved in with her. Ah well, better now than later.

"I am bringing in Madumo and Associates to investigate Allan and his affairs for my peace of my mind. Thanks for your time and listening ear dear. I must run."

Having made up her mind, Sonto determined to get to the bottom of the situation she found herself quickly. The man could kill her and quietly leave the country, never to be found again and no one would be the wiser or know how to trace him. It was amazing that during their time together she had never visited his home or probed more about his upbringing. Her approaching fiftieth birthday and lack of male companionship had made her desperate and lose track of personal safety and sensibilities. It was strange that a multimillionaire would see a need to take a lowly job at a construction site to enable him "to pay for my way and not be a burden". His earnings would not even cover their weekly groceries, what a mess.

They finished their food and Sonto called for their bill as she was now desperate to dig into Allan's life. She had made use of Madumo and Associates services before and appreciated their integrity, discreetness, and timeliness. They did not come cheap, but the cost would be worth it as the team consisted of former detectives and forensics experts. She headed home after her meeting and decided not to discuss the matter with Allan until the investigation had been concluded. She was going to continue with her self-imposed 'wifely' duties even in the bedroom so as to not raise any suspicion.

Keeping up the pretence proved challenging, but it was manageable as construction work kept Allan out of the house most of the time and he usually came back exhausted, ready to shower, eat and sleep. You could tell that he was not used to physical labour but enjoyed the company of other men and earning his keep.

"The work is quite hard, but the money is not bad…" Sonto choking on her lamb cutlet stopped Allan mid-sentence and brought him rushing to her assistance.

"Water, water please." He observed as she took gingerly sips in-between clearing her throat and wiping involuntary tears.

"Are you okay? Is there something bothering you? You seem a bit strained lately." Sonto frowned with concern at her carelessness, she had tried her utmost to act natural and she was not happy that Allan might have picked up something. She wanted him to stay in the dark until she had all the facts.

"Did Madumo and Associates finally locate you?" What the hell! Sonto willed every part in her body not to betray her whilst her brain scrambled furiously for answers.

"They are my attorneys, why and how do you know of them?" She asked and was relieved at the calmness in her voice.

"They called yesterday looking for you which I found odd, and I told them as much. Apparently, there was an urgent matter that required your attention, and they were battling to get hold of you." Lord take me now! What's wrong with these people and what a lame excuse. She needed a briefing with them immediately.

"I am sorry about that. That is unusual conduct for them. I will raise this matter with them and don't worry; they won't bother you again."

"Okay, thanks. So, is everything okay?"

"Yes dear. I was bogged down by year-end activities, but things are settling down and we will have time to revive our home search." Allan smiled and went back to his food.

The briefing with Madumo and Associates was quick and to the point. It turned out Allan was an imposter from Belarus who had fallen on hard times due to the on-going war between Russia and Ukraine which unbeknown to many had started in 2014. The investigators had managed to trace family members, friends, and business associates based on the telephone conversation they had with him while pretending to look for Sonto. They managed to access and mine crucial information through that call. Sonto did not understand half of the things they were mentioning but was glad that technology was bringing clarity to the matter. He had settled in the Bahamas having siphoned money from one of his business partner's accounts. The partner had tracked him down and received a court order to freeze his accounts, but he had managed to hightail himself to South Africa under an assumed name with limited funds, hence the current situation.

Sonto had met him during the tight financial squeeze and had provided the safe haven he so urgently needed so many miles away from home before his extradition could be completed. He had sought out other dubious compatriots who had created a base in Mzansi and were running 'legit' businesses used mostly for pimping or peddling purposes. The construction site job served as a lending base as he explored money making schemes to keep afloat.

"One of these include a marriage proposal during your birthday party." The investigator dropped this little nugget emotionlessly and proceeded to lay out some of the grander schemes Allan was cooking to live comfortably in this land of corruption, lawlessness, and greed.

"Oh really!" Bring it on Allan, I can't wait. Sonto left the offices of the investigators in high spirits having set-up an elaborate plan to bring Allan down to his knees.

"Hello Dora, I am good love. Listen, I need to add five additional guests on the list…" The rant and outrage from Dora could be heard from a distance but Sonto was determined to get whatever she wanted. It was her party after all.

"I can't get into the details right now, but it will be worth the effort. Believe me and the venue won't mind as we are bringing extra revenue. Also, the numbers are lower than the size of the venue." Sonto didn't understand what was frustrating Dora as all the work was being done by the event company and she was just facilitating the process for her.

"Sorry for the added stress my friend, I will call the company personally and handle any fallout that may arise…"

"No, no, no, I will do it. This is my duty. I was just surprised by this late notice." Sonto sighed with relief and thanked Dora for her understanding.

The big day finally dawned and found Sonto surrounded by her a make-up artist, a nail technician and her designer who doubled-up as her stylist. Her three cousins, Dora and her daughter were also present, and they were all taking turns being glammed up. Sonto had gone for a flowing ballgown dress in burgundy (her favourite colour), with diamond long dangle earrings in 18 carat white gold, subtle make-up, hair braided in up-style swept away from her face exposing her long regal neck, single diamond bracelet, gold box clutch bag with matching sandals to complete the look. A lot was at stake and riding on this single event, if she went down, it had to be in style. Dora was exquisite in a David Tlale black and gold ensemble accompanied by emerald earrings and pendant with matching heels and purse.

"Darling, the limousine has arrived." Allan poked his head to announce and departed hastily as if intimidated by a room full of women laughing and joking in languages still unfamiliar to his ears.

"Let's go ladies. We can't keep people waiting."

"Chill Sonto, it is your big day. You can afford to be late for once in your life." Sonto disagreed and stated that it could never be her. She considered deliberate lateness rude and disrespectful to guests or any person she had an appointment with.

Allan and Dora's husband were driving in front with three relatives, and they were following behind in a Limo. Sonto requested Dora to bless their journey and the upcoming festivities.

"Hawu kodwa Sonto, we arranged a priest nje for the festivities."

"Thandaza Dora and stop making excuses. I need a specific one, that we arrive safely, that all evil be revealed, and everything go as planned." Dora lunged into an impassioned prayer having detected anxiety and frustration in Sonto's voice.

The rest of the journey was completed in comfortable silence and anticipation of the night's event, Sonto's big day.

The Pheasant Hill Boutique Hotel provided the elegant charm, yet quaint and cosy ambience Sonto was aiming for her guests with plenty of room to move and mingle in the well-manicured gardens or the foyer.

Everyone looked amazing, the food was delicious, booze flowed, and the jazz band kept the guests bopping and swinging. The speeches were light, moving, whimsical or funny depending on the narrator. Dora had guests eating from the palm of her hands as she regaled on how they had met, their teen years and naughtiness, and what had kept them going all these years. Sonto reciprocated and they sealed their friendship with a toast.

Allan not to be outdone, stood up and toasted Sonto. He declared his admiration for her hardworking ethic and tenacity which "makes me love you more each day I spend with you and count myself lucky to have such a remarkable woman by my side".

It was a beautiful speech that got cheesier with each word and then every woman shrieked with delight as he whipped out an engagement ring and bent on one knee.

"Sonto, my dearest. It will be my honour and privilege if you would…"

"Not so fast maë kaxahhe…" Allan froze on the spot and turned slowly to face the woman who had seemed to appear from nowhere, his wife. He sprang

71

to action and sprinted for the door where he encountered three more unexpected and clearly unwelcomed individuals.

"Fedor, Yauheni, Aleh what are you guys doing here?" He turned to confront Sonto as the penny dropped because how else would these individuals have known his whereabout. He attempted to dart out of the other opening only to be confronted by security and one more unexpected guest, his business partner. Realising that his days as a fugitive were over, he faced Sonto again marvelling at how it took a mere woman to bring his running spree to a halt. She had been so desperate for a man that he became careless around her and missed the signs, the most important being the call from those lawyers. I should have listened to my instincts and paid more attention to what was happening around me, he mused.

Sonto watched without a tinge of regret as Allan was whisked away and concluded that being fifty and single was not such a bad thing as long as you had good people supporting and surrounding you. She was going to enjoy life with every fibre she had and would stop stressing about singlehood.

"Thank you everyone for coming and making my birthday celebrations such a wonderful and memorable occasion." Pausing briefly to catch her breath. "Please accept my sincere apologies for bringing chaos into your lives but I needed a cover to make the bust successful. Now let us have fun and be merry!"

They danced the night away with the band having retired and a vibrant DJ having taken over, Sonto felt relieved, fabulous, and great. *Hitting fifty was not so bad after all.*

The last she heard of Allan was that he had been beaten to a pulp and had been dropped at the nearest hospital by caring strangers who found him left for dead near some local sportsground. He was under police guard and awaiting deportation upon recovery, having survived death by a mere whisker.

Sonto learnt a valuable lesson that loneliness should never drive you to engage in desperate measures to catch a man. Ageing was supposed to bring maturity, wisdom and self-love, and not crazy teen behaviour which could have turned emotionally, physically, and financially costly. She was determined to go back to church and try dating again in the safety and sanctuary of the Lord.

IN HIS DARKEST HOUR

Themba had been walking aimlessly for two days away from his town of Pinetown without taking in his surroundings, stopping only to rest. Still traumatised by the sheer scale of devastation that the storm had wrought to his hometown. He felt angry at the government's lack of intervention which he had seen before where it had mobilised, with considered precision, emergency and humanitarian aid to neighbouring Mozambique a few years ago when that country had suffered similar devastation.

Where was the empathy and solidarity that had been shown to that country by the leaders? Why had it taken a few days before they could declare the floods a provincial disaster? Why had they not dispatched the army to immediately offer aid, leaving most of the task to the Gift of the Givers and individuals? Why was there calm and unhurried response in providing assistance to their own?

Recalling how he had watched helplessly as his house threatened to collapse under the sheer weight of gushing water that had approached from all angles made him choke with anguish. The contractor had been warned that the soil in that area was not suitable for urban planning. This warning fell on deaf ears as corrupt government officials and builders bulldozed their way in constructing the tiny houses and ran for the hills of Umhlanga Ridge to enjoy their bounty leaving people with shaky foundations. Though aware of the challenges in the area, Themba had been grateful to have a place of his own, especially when his father re-married for the fifth time, to a local beauty queen, who's desire was to keep the old man and his comfortable lifestyle all to herself.

His musings were distracted by a shadow in the corner of his eye. He retraced his steps when reality hit that he had gone farther than intended just as he noticed a red blob floating in the distance. He walked briskly along the road as he followed the blob and realised with shock that it was a car being carried away by the stream which flowed on the side of the road. He dialled the emergency number which had been provided to report sightings whilst hoping against hope that he had imagined seeing a human being in there. A voluntary shudder vibrated through his body as he thought about the condition they might be in if *there was indeed a human in there.* It seemed to Themba like ages before rescue workers made their way towards the area.

He flagged them urgently and pointed towards the direction of the car.

"It was a red car, and I might be wrong, but I think there was a person inside it." The sceptical look that passed between the rescue team made him question his own judgement, but he continued.

"I know what I saw. It is in your hands to do what you will with the information." Themba stated before turning on his heel with irritation at the timewasters.

"Sorry man, we didn't mean to challenge what you saw. Truth is we are overstretched and overworked. Further, we have dealt with a few false alarms in the last twelve hours." Themba shrugged as he wondered why these men were wasting more time on small talk instead of chasing the car.

"Come with us." Themba climbed on-board the emergency vehicle and the rescue team sped towards the direction of the car which was spotted later on heading towards a ravine. The crew quickly changed into their diving gear. Amazing, one minute they had seemed unbothered and disbelieving and the next minute they were moving at great speed to handle the situation, Themba observed with renewed hope.

The divers tied a rope on the grille of their bakkie and dived towards the floating car where they managed to fasten the end of the rope before instructing Themba 'to slam the accelerator whilst in reserve mode' which he did bringing the car back to dry land with such force that it landed with a bang. The car was foggy and Themba could just about pick-up a human shape inside. He wondered about his own state of mind when he had initially spotted the car and assumed that there was a person in there given the limited visibility at such close range.

Whimpering sounds beckoned from the car assuring him that the rescue mission might have been worth it. One of the rescue team members brought a crowbar and smashed the rear window to release the water and be able to open the car doors. Water came gushing out revealing sad and traumatic scenes for the crew and Themba who had been ordered to keep a distance.

Turned out that the driver had suffered a panic attack during the ordeal. The dog had survived and kept guard over its owner throughout the incident. The rescue team assumed that the man might be in the missing persons' list and/or not yet accounted for. They needed to notify the authorities who will then try to locate his relatives.

Themba urged closer to the car as the crew wrestled the dog from the car. He peered over the crews' heads and gazed into the dog's eyes. Its defeated and melancholy gaze tugged at his heartstrings and all the emotions of the past few days came rushing through, bringing mournful sobs. An overwhelmed Themba left the car and scampered away as the impact of his own loss threatened to overshadow the moment.

Strangled sounds filled his ears and dragged him back to the scene. The crew parted as he approached, and the dog voluntarily raised its paws towards him. He scooped it as it threw itself willingly towards his open arms and snuggled comfortably against his shoulders heaving with unshed tears. He brushed, soothed, and agonised with the dog.

"Dude, the dog has adopted you." A crew member muttered more to himself than to him. Themba nodded slightly.

"Come with us so we can lodge a formal statement with the police, and we will then take you home---" Pausing unsure and staring at his colleagues as Themba howled openly.

"I aaaaam sorrrrry about that. It is just that the floods hit my home hard. I have been walking aimlessly for the last two days. You just brought home the fact that I might have no place to go to and would need to find shelter for me and the dog."

"Oh, that's rough. What about your family?"

"They live far from here. I can't keep the dog."

"We will provide shelter for you and the dog for the next few days until we can locate the deceased's family." Looking at his colleague for concurrence before proceeding. "You and the dog have been through a lot and need each other."

Themba just nodded and followed the crew to their bakkie with his new friend firmly cuddled in his chest. He made use of the telephone at the police station to update his employer on his whereabouts and to officially request time off, only to be informed that the store had been flooded and would be closed for a while. He was assured that they would be compensated for the next couple of months and would be informed of the return date once the shop was running again. Themba wondered around the station uncertain of what the future held for him and his companion.

"Are you good mate?" Asked a crew member and he just smiled wearily.

"Let's go. We have found shelter for you guys." Sighing with relief, Themba picked the dog and went to the waiting car.

"We also managed to locate the deceased's family, unfortunately, most of them live outside the country but they have promised to come through on Friday or latest Saturday depending on how quickly they can finalise their travel arrangements."

They were taken to the outskirts of Umzinto where the crew had managed to secure him a bunk bed in a pet-friendly backpacking hostel. The owner had two dogs of her own and was only too happy to provide free lodgings and food for them.

The sister to the deceased man landed on Saturday morning and headed straight to the funeral parlour for identification before proceeding to the hostel to meet with Themba and re-unite with the dog which she had met on several visits to her younger brother who had opted to stay in the country when everybody in the family, including his two kids, emigrated to different parts of Europe.

"Pleased to meet you Themba. I am Margrieta, David's sister. I heard how you discovered his car. Thank you so much."

"You are welcome, although I didn't do much except call the emergency crew."

"Exactly that, otherwise we might not have found them." Unsure how to proceed further, Themba let the matter rest. Margrieta informed him that the rest of the family would be landing on Monday and had requested that she takes care of all the funeral arrangements as the first person to land in the country. She invited Themba to attend the service, which was set for the coming Wednesday, but he felt obliged to decline as he didn't know the deceased nor his family.

Margrieta implored with him to attend, stating that the dog would need a familiar figure and a companion. Themba eventually agreed to attend the funeral service and informed Margrieta that it might serve as an opportune moment to part ways with the dog amongst familiar faces and surroundings, even though it saw the family members at irregular intervals.

Early Monday morning found Themba in a taxi on his way to his old dwelling to see if he could salvage something to wear at the funeral. Arriving at the sight brought fresh perspective of the disaster that had befallen them. He was surprised to find that most structures had survived and that his own home, although it was slightly buried and tilting but was still accessible. He bumped into a neighbourhood friend who had managed to scrape through his home once the land dried down a bit and had salvaged a few of his items which he had stored for him. Themba was touched by the generosity and humanity shown towards him and those around him when everybody had been impacted negatively by the storms.

He thanked him and managed to pull together a decent outfit for the funeral and the friend agreed to accompany him as he felt uncomfortable attending a stranger's funeral alone. Themba and the dog stayed at the friend's place so they could travel together to the funeral. The service was short and beautiful, and they were requested to assemble at the hall for refreshments after the service. Margrieta introduced them to the rest of the family which thanked Themba profusely for his intervention.

A short meeting was held with him where the family requested that he continued taking care of the dog and offered him the use of their unoccupied cottage which the family owned outside Pinetown, and a handsome amount of money to look after himself and the dog. It turned out that other than the dog and the local Priest, the deceased had no friends in the area. Everyone agreed that the dog through its owner's spirit had adopted Themba as its new master. The matter was settled with no further discussion. Themba's 'intuition' and warm heart had turned out to be the biggest blessing he could ever had asked for. A misfortune had been turned around by an act of kindness, where being at the right place and at the right time and having the presence of mind to intervene accordingly had saved the day. Themba named the dog Musa with a thankful heart that acknowledged that mercy had been bestowed upon him in his darkest hour.

Themba volunteered his services to the rescue team and Musa was trained as a rescue dog to assist in helping others who might find themselves in desolate and/or unfortunate conditions to get the necessary intervention on time. New family bonds were established. Tragedy was turned into everlasting friendships and adventurous times.

SPIRIT OF THE DEAD

The horse plodded through the snow at an alarmingly slow pace as if carrying the burdens of the world. Doug couldn't get it to move any faster, try as much as he could. In a way he understood its protest, they had been on the road for the past four months having started with a crew of eight strong men and had been reduced to two. The horse had been baked and frozen and couldn't take it anymore.

They had been excited at the prospect of striking it rich and coming back to gloat in the face of all those that had dared to call them 'good for nothing scumbags". What hurt the most was Doug's wife leading the chorus of people who thought they were an embarrassment. Apparently, they couldn't be classified as bandits, cowboys, or anything worthy.

They had embarked on this treacherous trip to seek gold deemed to be scattered around the Rocky Mountains after bandits attacked a prospecting banker four years ago. The bandits has been on the run from the law for two years when they chanced upon the banker and his workers on their way to the bank. The banker had stumbled upon a conversation of gold discovery at a town saloon he was visiting.

The place had been abuzz with prophetic allusions of gold in the area with most patrons scoffing at the idea of riches hiding within their reach all these years without a sighting. They had all agreed that it was a hoax and that the boy who started the rumours needed to be taught a lesson to stop lying. The saloon had belonged to the boy's father who was under extreme pressure to discipline him or allow the locals to flog him. The banker did his utmost best to hide his excitement at the news and pounced immediately when there was a lull in the discussion.

"Gentlemen, you sure have a mighty problem in your hands." He chimed in during a lull. Eyes turned towards him assessing his look and was found wanting judging by the unimpressed and condescending faces turned towards him.

"I'm prepared to go with the boy to test his prophesy and you can give him a beating if we find nothing." He continued nonchalantly unaffected by their confusion. The men were unsure whether to declare him insane or stupid.

"It best you don't involve yourself in this matter. We don't want no trouble. You, city slickers tend to create unnecessary bag of nails. Where you from mister, you look like you belong in a bank." A ruddy faced fellow in bright yellow breeches and brown dungarees spoke for the group.

"Yeh, you right Jim. He ain't from these parts, looking all dandy..."

"I mean no harm gentlemen. Let the boy take me to the spot and I will return him unharmed with or without the gold. You can sort him out if required then."

"What do we do about you?"

"Nothing, I am giving a solution to your challenge." The banker was eager to move, as the idea of making it big meant he could finally ask for Clarissa's hand in marriage. Currently, Mr. Sous did not consider him husband material as he worked at his bank, and he treated him like one of the hired hands.

The men conferred and decided the wait will be more satisfactory as they will get to flog the boy and the city slicker for his interference on local matters. So it was that the banker, the boy, and the crew he had assembled the previous day set off early in the morning in search of gold. The county deemed it unnecessary to provide mining permits as everyone was convinced that it was going to be a useless exercise and they couldn't wait to see the stranger eat humble pie.

It took the crew eleven days to reach the supposed mining sight and they could see from a distance a sparkling shimmer of what looked like mineral deposits peeking from the ground. They rested for the night and got to work digging very early the next day. They worked daily until they reached the first proper metals and placed these in a shed they had erected. The mining area was in a semi-arid area, and it got mighty hot during the day and very cold at night. The banker stuck to a five AM to one PM and three PM to eight PM schedule to protect them from the harsh conditions.

They started with detonations on the tenth day to enable them to go deeper. He rode to the nearest town with two of his crew members to source encampment material to protect them from bandits.

Word spread of his findings and groups of men started plotting ways to relieve him of his gold on his way to the bank, which was expected to happen soon. They let him continue with the dirty work and persuaded one of the crew members to provide them with reports on progress. A jolly Christmas was to be had.

Word reached him of the plots. He decided to bring extra security and transport what they had excavated earlier than planned. He sourced cowboys from one of the nearest towns to accompany him. He left the boy and a foreman in charge and departed very early that morning with as much gold as he could load in the stagecoach he had rented. The trip started well until they were halfway through, when suddenly, they saw bandits approaching at highspeed heading their way. Gunshots rang out and the cowboys flanking the stagecoach returned fire with fire. The coachman did all he could to calm the horses to no avail. They got spooked and bolted leaving the banker trapped in the runaway coach which careened for miles before crashing and plunging down the mountain to the ravine below with most of the gold and the banker who was killed instantly.

The cowboys made off and headed back to the mining camp with the bandits in hot pursuit.

"Incoming, lock the gates. Lock the gates, there is trouble coming."

The crew rushed to shut the rickety gates once the cowboys were safely inside with gunpowder racketing non-stop. There were more bodies scattered around than gold by the end of that evening. The remaining men made their way to the digging site the following day only to find it completely covered with snow. It was quite a strange sight as it continued to snow incessantly over that part of the land and nowhere else. The crew abandoned all effort to dig for more gold after four weeks of constant snow and dwindling supplies. They made off with the little pile that was still in the shed which was woefully just enough to be shared amongst them all but not bring much riches as predicted.

"Let's rather retrace the banker's steps and see if we can't find left over gold there." One of the crew members ventured as the futility of their hard work lay achingly tattered.

"Agreed." A few crew members and the cowboys left the site and headed on horseback towards the crash site and were never to be seen again. They disappeared into thin air on top of what turned out to be a dangerous and treacherous mountain.

Word spread like fire that the banker and his crew had gone down, and many a man trudged towards the crash site hoping to salvage something. Many reached the crash site but were never seen again while others gave up just days before reaching the area. Rumours started swirling around that the place was haunted with most returnees claiming to have encountered a vicious spirit. They stated that the banker seemed to have died holding on to his bounty with eyes haunted by the horror of his impending doom. It became clear that no one was going to retrieve the gold from the crash site nor excavate further. The banker had died a horrific death after depositing much sweat equity towards the gold site and was not gonna let lazy buggers try to rob him of his hard-earned bounty.

Well, that was so until Doug heard of the story and thought he was man enough to tackle the challenge.

Doug had been married for more than twenty years and in all those years had endured humiliation and made to feel worthless. Nothing he did was good enough for his wife who blamed her parents for marrying her off to a "lowlife, weakling." The constant badgering grew worse over the years and seemed to rub off on the children. Nothing he did was ever taken seriously or appreciated. He saw this as an opportunity to prove himself worthy and break free from the bonds of family.

He could still hear his wife's scornful laughter when she heard one of his friends casually mention their upcoming trip, buoyed by excitement at what lay instore for them.

"What, you gotta be kidding! My Doug going on an expedition! A life and death expedition for that matter, not happening. Hahaha."

Initially Doug was unsure himself if he could carry out such an endeavour, but the continued jabs forced him off his comfort zone and led him to this godforsaken place.

The first few weeks were relaxed as they would wake up to hearty breakfast, fed the horses and hit the road.

93

The weather changed up a notch along the way, but they could still handle it. They persevered and continued with the trip but halfway through a blinding blizzard hit them hard and they were forced to lay low. Two of his friends suffered from hypothermia and they had to devise means to warm them up so the cold could not strike and kill them. No sooner had they recovered, with snow now gone, when one of them forgot to check his boots before putting them on and got bitten by a snake. Things seemed to go downhill from then on as they got closer to their destination.

Hallucinations, diarrhoea, severe snow, and attacks led by unseen creatures which left three of the men mutilated convinced them that they were dealing with evil spirits. The remaining friends bade him farewell and went back home, leaving Doug and Peet, who was either stupid or brave enough, to see the journey through.

Peet's horse caved in on the last night and folded right there, and they had to take turns riding Doug's horse which was also on its last legs. That's how we found them traipsing ever so slowly towards their destination with Doug mounted on his horse and Peet following on foot at a distance.

A gust of wind arose from nowhere and lashed quite hard. He heard Peet screaming for help, and he yelled at him to drop on his stomach, hoping the wind would carry the message through to him. He heard footsteps approaching quite fast and moved out of the way just in time as a booted leg landed where he was.

"Who's you?" A voice from the depths of his being demanded.

"The owner of this area. I am tired of you people chasing me even in death."

Was that the banker's ghost? Doug wandered.

"Sorrrrry mister. We mean no harm. We just want a share of gold."

"No one believed the boy except me and now you wanna claim what you didn't work for. Ain't happening."

That is fair, thought Doug but he also knew that he was not leaving without that bounty.

"We have travelled from far and are asking for a few metals, please mister?"

"Quite insistent, ain't you? No one has made it this far except you two."

"That should count for something right?"

Doug dared to look up but there is no one. He shivered as he realised that he was indeed conversing with the departed.

"What do you want mister?" Doug asked.

"I wanna go home. I need to rest, can you help? I have been out here too long waiting for the one."

"Yes, I can mister, but I don't know how."

"I will guide you through the Passover ritual."

"Okay."

You can then carry my spirit home with whatever bounty you can collect and carry."

"Why are you trusting me with this process?"

"You made it thus far and you seem to care, I can see it."

So it was that Doug and Peet collected the bounty and headed home with the banker's spirit. He protected them all the way and no one dared touch them or attempt to rob them of their bounty. Doug and Peet received a hero's welcome. However, they could no longer settle in a town that had belittled them. They used their fortunes to explore and discover the world at leisure without bickering and scornful wives after laying the banker where he belonged.

GO OUT IN STYLE

The chants and singing were barely audible but there was no mistaking that distinct toyi-toyi rhythm. This moment had been a long time coming and it seemed like this was it. Every fibre and whisker in him confirmed that the frenzied crowd was headed their way. Percy watched Malebo, his mistress, from his comfy snuggle place as she shuffled to her bedroom with muscles tensed up and taut like a guitar string. He figured that she had also picked up the sounds and he wanted to shout, "this is not the time to hide!" She had been harassed and sworn at in the past few years he had been with her that he desired for her to take a stand.

He begrudgingly followed her to the bedroom but stopped in his tracks as she emerged from the room holding a Smeg box, the most expensive thing she had splurged on this past year. He wanted to clap in appreciation as the moment deserved "a yes baby, let's go out in style".

The vocal singing was getting closer and was indeed headed their way, *must be quite a crowd*. The melodies were to die for, pity as this was not the time nor place to appreciate the melodious voice of the lead singer who kept the crowd going. Fuelling its anger with promises of agonising death for "the witch who had been terrorising the neighbourhood for years".

"It was time for revenge and retribution for all the atrocities and misery she had inflicted on the community". There were cries of remembered pain, loss, and mutual sentiment to "finally deal with the pandemic that had caused untold misery amongst the people of Majabana Township".

Percy watched his mistress unhurriedly remove the kettle from the box, fill it with water before plugging it. She retrieved two of her special cups from the sideboard, these were usually reserved for those rare occasions when the Pastor popped by. Percy observed this strange conduct and was even more surprised when she brought side plates and loaded them up with her best cookies. She warmed milk and filled one cup with it and topped the other cup with coffee and water.

It suddenly dawned on him that the milk arrangement was for him just as she beckoned that he joined her in the dining table. She stroked his fur gently rousing pure enjoyment whilst at the back of his head, he wondered why she had never shown this side of her before. Her aloof manner and seemingly uncaring demeanour had cemented the rumours swirling in the neighbourhood that she was abducting young boys for witchcraft practices. Her saving grace was that no one had caught her in the act yet and the sedate pristine white cat which didn't fit the narrative of 'witches' cats which tended to be black with a mean disposition.

Percy noticed that the crowd had now assembled at their gate with the leaders caucusing and he thought it best to crouch closer so he can follow the discussions.

"Percy, come back. It's dangerous out there." Her voice trembling with anxiety. Percy stepped out with renewed vigour as he needed to know their fate and the reasons for this visit. He recognised Ms Xulu's voice (mortuary owner), her son Smiley, and another unknown female voice.

"Comrades, there is no need to engage further. Let us burn the house and watch her die inside. Also, it will be quicker to disburse if the police decide to show up." Smiley.

"No son, I want to see her face as we put the tyre around her and light the matches. People have lost kids and relatives and now she dares attack me in my home. The witch must feel our pain!" Ms Xulu.

"I hear you, but we have no proof that she committed these atrocities. Also, Ms Xulu there have been rumours around your mortuary business…" Unknown voice.

"How dare you?"

"Well, it's true but we digress. People have been making these accusations against Malebo for a while just because she keeps to herself…"

"And owns a cat. Anyway, we have left her alone until now. Two neighbours were attacked by zombies in the last few weeks that disappeared to this house."

"Did anyone here see them enter this house?" Few heads bobbed unconvincingly, and Ms Xulu felt compelled to vocally claim that she saw them but was too scared to come forward until this morning when she found one under her bed.

"Mama came out screaming and we fled. Enough talking let's go in."

Percy decided he had had enough as the crowd got more vocal than those who had called for the Lord's crucifixion. They were getting frustrated with the dithering and wanted action and were now forcefully pulling at the locked gate.

His mistress grabbed and cuddled him as he entered through the door flap. She apologised for her conduct in the past and implored that he leaves before the crowd came in as she didn't want his death on her conscious. She gently placed him down and fetched the gate keys, but Percy stopped her as she turned the doorknob.

"Mistress! It does not have to end this way..." Stupid me, he thought as he stood licking and fanning her in his attempt to wake her up as she had collapsed from the shock of hearing him talk. The timing was wrong as he needed her awake to carry out his plans. He was sent to guard her with express instructions to hide his powers. Ah well, second option it is. There was no time to waste as the crowd had managed to rip the gate apart and was now in the yard and headed towards the house.

Percy howled terrifyingly to stall the crowd whilst summoning Malebo's ancestors to step forth and take control. The crowd heard him, and half of them took off whilst others excited with the thought of catching the witch red-handed charged forward and broke down the kitchen door. The first ones through the door watched in shock and horror as they found the cat submerging itself and getting consumed by the "witch" as she lay unconscious on the floor. She twitched vigorously as the cat disappeared inside her and then rose like a charged bull as her body underwent various transformations before she finally landed on all fours looking feral and majestic.

The guttural wolf's cry that filled the tiny four-roomed house left no one in doubt that it meant business. Some stood transfixed whilst others ran for dear life. The wolf prowled up and down the small dining room, sniffing and circling them and finally settled on Smiley who was spotting fresh pee.

The merged duo of Percy and his mistress commanded Smiley, Ms Xulu and the remaining comrades to lead them to the Xulu's home. Percy was partially upset to have revealed his powers in this manner having done his utmost best to hide his identity to date, but it had to be done. He had been resurrected from the dead by Malebo's ancestors and was given transformative powers before making his way to her home as a lost cat and getting himself adopted against her will. This was done to protect her from the narrow-minded and mean community averse to newbies.

She had come to this town to heal and start afresh from past tragedies, but the community had been unwelcoming to the beautiful and independent person who required nothing from them except shelter big enough to cater for her needs.

Unfortunately, a few months after moving in young boys started disappearing without a trace. Ms Xulu started whispering false narratives about their disappearances which eventually raised enough suspicion to put a spotlight on the poor woman. The fact that none of the neighbours could link the boys' disappearance with the opening of a mortuary in the same vicinity that seemed to boom instantly, an act that was normally tied to ritual killings to bring more wealth, was puzzling to Percy.

To make matters worse, a couple of years later neighbours started experiencing strange occurrences like sightings of zombies in the neighbourhood which were being used as slaves (apparently by his mistress), a naked woman flying with a broom at night sprinkling evil spirits resulting in miscarriages, massive job losses, hallucinations, unexplainable diseases, and husbands deserting 'happy' marriages. Ms. Xulu had claimed that this indicated that the witch's strength and superpowers were growing.

That is when coordinated and abusive attacks intensified to the extent that Malebo stopped going out and Percy was woken up after years of slumber to be with her so he can intervene whenever required. He had been able to fend minor attacks so far without exposing himself, but today's invasion had necessitated a bold intervention. He sensed that the visit to Ms Xulu's home would expose many ills so his mistress could be absolved from the lies, and he could rest in peace.

Ms Xulu's house was a couple of houses from his mistress' home, and he was glad to find the gate wide open as they approached. Ms Xulu was ordered to lead the way as Percy wanted her by his side when they entered her room. Smiley and the few remaining community members were instructed to come with. There was a slight hesitation, but he would have none of it. He growled his instructions again whilst threatening to sink his fangs on any non-compliant person's throat. This moved them to action, and they tumbled in with lots of shoving as none of them wanted to be in front.

He was not sure what to expect but was prepared for it. They entered through the kitchen and wove their way down the small passage. The place deserved its own channel to showcase the filth and rot inside. There was dirt and dust everywhere which he had never come across in all his years on planet earth, dirty dishes everywhere in the kitchen with the sink overflowing. Rats and cockroaches scuttled away shocked by the intrusion as the group made its way to the main bedroom. Sneezes, snuffles, and gagging formed a chorus as people battled to breath. The sitting room was covered with cobwebs, and you could see dust piled up high. A sneeze voluntarily made its way through his nostrils as the dust tickled his nostrils but there was no turning back. He instructed Ms Xulu to open the door, but she stood there fearful of the dangers lurking inside and the task was left to Smiley.

He gingerly opened the door and tried to flee but Percy gripped his ankle tightly forcing a painful wail. He eventually loosened his grip and nuzzled him inside as he followed behind. Everyone else congregated near the door ready to bolt as Percy worked his way towards the bed covered all the way to the floor by a bedspread that had seen better days. He muttered a few words and the bedspread moved on its own volition, and people screamed in terror at the monster lying underneath.

"You see, we told you. The witch went straight for it. We should have killed her..." said one of the onlookers.

"Stop being dramatic. Come and have a look before you make more unfounded accusations against my mistress." Growled an irritated Percy.

They stood motionless whilst Ms Xulu backed away. It was obvious that the room had not been cleaned in years and dust had collected to the point where it took a 'monster's shape. They were also shocked to see human bones peeking out, and all turned accusing eyes towards Smiley as Ms Xulu had bolted. Whatever had prompted the Percy and Malebo combo to search underneath the bed had spooked Ms Xulu to an extent that she had unwittingly exposed herself. It was bewildering though that someone in

Ms Xulu's position could live like that, in sheer squalor whilst portraying a glamourous life in public.

The community stood ashamed and unable to face Malebo as she was transformed back to human form with Percy exiting her body to retain his feline state.

"Let's go home Percy. We have high tea to finish."

She lovingly scooped him up but stopped immediately as she wondered why she had never paid attention to his eyes, her deceased husband's eyes.

"Mam' Malebo?"

"I would like to extend my apologies on behalf of the community for the manner in which we have treated you all these years. We are sorry and hope you will find it in you to forgive us at some point."

She did not know how to respond to that and so just nodded and left to live her new life with Percy, her darling hubby whom she would always love in whatever form he showed himself for as long as she shall live. Her wonderful saviour.

THE OBSESSION

Hello?" I answered cautiously. After all this is still the house of the Lord even though the service is being conducted in a school hall due to the numbers. The local church branch can only accommodate fifty parishioners and we would not have fitted given that this is a provincial easter Sunday service. Quite impressive that a local school has such facilities given where we come from as a black community of conquered and divided South Africa.

"I am outside."

"Outside where?" There is no way…

"Your home?" Heaving slightly, I quickly go on high alert. Why?

"What are you doing there?" Surely, he did not go there.

"To see you of course." With slight irritation at my response.

"But I mentioned that I will be attending church this weekend."

"Yes, that was yesterday which is why I did not bother you." I need to take this outside. Heads are starting to turn my way and I catch a disapproving glance from mom on the corner of my eye. Our daughter is still sleeping peacefully on the sleeping bag I laid down for her on the floor. I can hear heavy breathing on the phone. He is probably getting upset at my silence.

"I will call just now. Bye." I whisper before dropping the call. Probably not the wisest decision but I can't be doing this during a church service. It seems disrespectful to the women gathered in front reciting the last seven words before the Lord took his last breath. I wait until they are finished before heading out. The phone has not stopped vibrating ever since I dropped the call unceremoniously. I am disturbed by all this.

I slip the phone surreptitiously inside my church jacket before letting mom know that I am going to the bathroom and requesting that she keeps an eye on the baby whilst I am gone. She nods suspiciously but I am gone before she can question me. One thing about my mom is that she does not miss a thing, like most caring moms I suppose.

I answer the call before I even reach the door. It is his seventh one since I dropped the call. This is starting to freak me out now. I am at church for Christ's sake what is all this fuss about.

"Hello?"

"Why did you take this long to call me back?"

"I was waiting for the maanyano ladies to finish reading the scripture."

"Where is Luthando?"

"She is sleeping. Her lights went out a couple of hours ago?"

"Sleeping where?"

"In a sleeping bag." Why am I even out here responding to random questions when I should be inside there singing my favourite sefela. I can hear mme Maki's voice leading that calvary song as she only could, and church members are feeling it. Their voices rise in unison and blend beautifully with the

111

lead vocalist. I start swaying to the beat, feeling the holy spirit taking over me until I am brought back by his voice. Yhoo haaikhona madoda this is too much.

"When are you coming back?"

"Tomorrow morning?"

"Why? Are you working nightshift now. I thought church runs only during the day…" This is starting to irritate me.

"As mentioned in our discussion…"

"Discussion with who?"

"With you. When we were talking about our plans for the easter weekend." I need to calm down and be rational. I must not let him get to my head or I will lose it and forget what this weekend means to me. Easter weekend has always been a sacred space for me where I get reminded of what Christ sacrificed for us sinners to have everlasting life. I have been coming to these services for the past fifteen years without fail and all this was clarified from the beginning of our relationship four years ago and I thought it was understood as there has never been problems so far.

"No, I don't remember. I just know that you went to church yesterday. Today's event is news to me." Counting to ten before responding seems a better option.

"I am sorry love. I did mention this trip on Thursday. I should have reminded you again this morning."

"Okay."

"I need to go back." Relieved that we may, for now, put this matter to rest.

"Are you going in there to pack for your return?" What? No! What medicine is this guy on?

"No, I am going back to check on Luthando and continue with the service."

"What about me?" Dear holy Moses! Please raise thy rod again right now.

"Well---. You can go home or come join us. It will take you about an hour to get here given the lateness of the hour." There should be minimal cars on the road at eleven PM on Holy Saturday.

"I don't appreciate your sarcasm." Hhawu, that was a genuine statement.

"I was not being sarcastic. I am sorry if it came out that way. Look I have to go. Mom will be serving me bitter words if I am gone for too long, especially with the kid unattended to…"

"She is the grandmother. She can take care of the child."

"It is not her baby or her responsibility."

"You are too soft. That is what grandparents are there for Thabi. To take care and look after the grandchildren."

"I really must go now. We will chat tomorrow morning..."

"Wait, what don't you leave the baby there. You can fetch it in the morning."

"What?" I don't know which part of the conversation this man is not understanding. I am here to worship and praise. I ain't going nowhere until morning.

"Yes, we will get to spend alone time together without worrying about the baby."

"That is not happening. Bye babes."

I drop the call before he can respond and go back. Mama gives me the look but holds her tongue as the preacher is now on-stage imparting words of encouragement and wisdom.

The phone starts vibrating as soon as I sit down. This time I ignore it completely and throw it inside my handbag which I put on the floor next to Luthando. I immerse myself in the word and fellowship. It is not until two-thirty AM that I retrieve it out of curiosity more than anything else during tea break. I have eight missed calls since we last spoke and the phone vibrates again just as I attempt to listen to the recorded message left ten minutes earlier. I answer the call and fortunately mama has left for the bathroom and the other ladies we came with are helping themselves at the tea station.

"Why did you not answer my calls?" He shouts angrily before I can respond. I almost jump from my seat at the change of tone.

"Because I am at church." What is wrong with this guy?

"But I am waiting."

"You are still outside my place?"

"Yes."

"But why?"

"That is a stupid question." Breath Thabi, breath. This man is testing me. I am going to start cussing very soon if we carry on. I can feel it. People expect churchgoers to behave like sheep and not have feelings. They think they can do, say and walk all over us without retaliation because we are praise singers. Let us be honest. There is only one man who spoke of and believed that you should offer your other cheek whilst being pounded and skinned, mina I am the 'an-eye-for-an-eye' kind of person. That is why church is so important to me. It serves as my confessional and release space where I offload my week's mischiefs so I can start afresh and deal with more nonsense that may come my way.

I have seen flashes of this behaviour before but have always managed to squash it before it became a thorn in the flesh. Initially I was ordered to stop meeting with my friends because "we are too old now to be grooving and staying out until late at night." Then it was "why do you still need to travel for work at your level" to "why are you travelling with a male colleague, aren't there female colleagues?"

I addressed these very quickly but there have been others that I have ignored. Tonight's conduct is unbecoming and has reached annoyance proportions. I don't like the rabbit hole he is taking me to. I need my anointing and forgiveness of sin so I can start on a new slate for this coming year. Can't we wait until tomorrow night for this nonsense? I need my blessings right now.

"Thami, I need to go now, I am done with this." I firmly hang up and put my phone on flight mode where it should have been after the first conversation. I cannot trace exactly when this conduct started again but judging by today's interaction, it seems to be steadily growing and getting out of hand. Who camps at someone's place for the night knowing full well that they are at church with their kid and mom.

Service resumes shortly after the last call. I focus my energies on the scriptures and worshipping. We all wait in anticipation for the five AM slot where we will march in the streets with the brass band announcing His resurrection and triumph over death. I feel rather than see him. Oh wow, he has decided to join the service. This is hectic. I didn't expect that knowing full well his aversion to church and was actually joking when I mentioned that he should come. He has no qualms with the Lord but has an unfathomable detestation for church buildings and the leadership surrounding them. It is like he carries festered wounds that refuse to heal.

"What is he doing here?" Mama has spotted him, aaii this is not going to end well.

"Who mama?" I ask innocently. I am just buying time here.

"Your control freak. You need to break-up with that man before it is too late."

"What do you mean?"

"You know exactly what I am talking about. I have been observing you since you gave birth. You have become a shadow of your old self." This is serious. Even my family have noticed the changes and him being here is going to make matters worse. Yah, it is time to act.

"You are right mama. It is time I ended it."

"Not here though dear. We don't want drama." Of course not. I thought she knows me better than that.

I observe him from the corner of my eye for the duration of the service. Initially he just stands there texting and calling to no avail as my phone is still off. Someone provides him with their spare hymn book. He eventually joins in the proceedings as he knows full well that he can't approach me with mom here. There is hostilities between them. She has never liked him "there is darkness underneath that charm Thabi, please tread carefully" she warned me on their first meeting and her views have never changed. He has just confirmed that and raised her views of him to paranoid levels this morning.

Service concludes with a hymn and a prayer at six AM. We decide to head home and not wait for breakfast. Mama is still feeling vulnerable after the loss of my stepfather two years earlier. This is her first church outing since then and she has decided not to stay for the morning service even though we both would have wanted to partake in holy communion. I pack up Luthando's things and we say our goodbyes to our fellow congregants before going to the car. I see his car, but I cannot locate him. I load our things in the boot of the car and remove flight mode in my phone. A flood of missed calls and messages beep through which I ignore. I leave a message informing him that we have left. I am heading to Protea North to drop mom and I suggest we meet there. Safety in numbers will be required when I break the news that we can no longer be a couple. I am done, tonight was the last straw.

We detour via Southgate Mall to buy MacDonald breakfast and coffee for us, my two brothers at home and him. There is no way we are cooking after an all-night service. All we need now is food, shower, and bed in that exact order. We find him already parked on the side of the road. I use the remote to open the gate and the garage before gliding in. He follows and parks inside the gate. I close the gate and we all proceed to the house where we eat in silence. I invite him to join me and Luthando in my room at home, which is situated outside, next to the outside bathroom which separates my room and that of my older brother.

"Please take a seat." I hasten to add before he closes in for a kiss. He throws me a peculiar look but proceeds to take a seat at the edge of the bed. I sit facing him on the only chair in the room. I want eye contact so he can know that I mean business.

"I can't do this anymore Thami."

"What do you mean?" He asks softly, dangerously so.

"The constant calls and checking up on me I could tolerate. However, last night showed me that we have reached dangerous levels in this relationship. I am done."

He laughs softly without any humour before stating that he is not going anywhere.

"This my relationship Thabi, my relationship! It will end when I say so…"

"Is there a problem here?" That's how loud it got we didn't even hear my brother come in.

"Cha, bhuti. UThami is on his way out. We are done."

"Oh okay." My brother opens the door wide, indicating to Thami that it was time for him to leave. He gives me a scary look before heading for the door. He knows he is outnumbered here. Besides my brother is known for his tendencies to rough people up and I think he is secretly scared of him. I can tell though that this is not over by a longest shot.

"Are you alright sisi?"

"Yebo bhuti. I just need to take a shower and nap. It has been a long night." I mean it and feel the statement in every fibre of my body.

"Okay, let me know if lenja ikuhlupha."

"Kulungile bhuti, I will.".

"You are mine. I am not going anywhere. That is the end of the story." His message beeps through ominously which I show to my brother. He calls Thami immediately and tells him to back off if he doesn't want trouble.

Days pass without a word until I start receiving flowers daily on my porch without a written note. I love flowers and I keep them until I get a niggling suspicion that they might be from him. I bar the delivery man from bringing them from thereon, but he shows up constantly until I re-direct him to the funeral parlour to offer them as a donation to needy families who have lost their loved ones and cannot afford flowers. This seems to bother Thami, and he retaliates by calling at awkward times waking Luthando up. I resort to switching my phone off in the evenings which leads him to following me everywhere and leaving handwritten notes on my doorstep and windscreen professing his love. This conduct is starting to freak me out and mama recommends putting in place a restraining order.

This seems to work for a while until this fateful day when he rocks up at work and charms the security lady to letting him in unannounced. I have not informed any of my colleagues and employer about the restraining order which has led to him easily gaining access to my office and barricading us inside.

"The game is over Thabi."

"What do you mean?"

"I told you I am not going anywhere. I have given you time to come to your senses, but you are not taking me seriously. You need to learn a lesson."

He places the bag he is carrying on my table and out comes a powdery portion, Vaseline jelly, cottonwool, razorblades, iziqhaza…

"What are you planning to do with these things Thami?" A devilish smile curls around his lips before he responds.

"To brand you, my love." I dial security as his intentions become clearer. He rips the phone and its cord before I can utter a word.

"What do you mean?" I have to keep him talking whilst I figure a way out of here.

"When I am done with piercing your ears no man will want to touch you but me."

Oh, my word. He is going to slice my ears and insert the Zulu props (iziqhaza) which will stretch my earlobes to dangling proportions. No ways. I would rather die than have those. There is no way I am going to have hanging earlobes. There is going to be war and blood will be spilled in this office. One thing I am certain of is that he will touch my ears over my dead body not whilst I am still breathing.

I position myself near my bag and wait for him to attack. I don't want him to see it coming. He is done preparing the blade and lunges for my head ready to slice. I evade him just in time and tase him good for a couple of minutes until he goes lame. I unlock the door and scream for help at the top of my lungs. Security comes barging in and subdue him further before calling the police. A case of attempted bodily harm and breaking the restraint order is brought against him.

He gets thrown in jail with a pimp who has an affinity for cute men, unfortunately, for him. The last I heard he was headed for the looney house as he had difficulty comprehending and dealing with the molestation. Guilt hits me from time-to-time, after all he is my babby daddy, until mama reminds me of the danger I escaped from.

The funny thing is that Thami had lost all interest in me six months into my pregnancy. He still came occasionally to check on me but would not stay for long or even touch me. It had seemed as if I ceased to exist in his eyes during that period until three months after giving birth.

Luthando was colic and put me through hell in the first few weeks of being born. I lost all the baby fat and some. By the time I went for my post-pregnancy check-up I was weighting fifty-one kilograms from a heavy hundred and twenty. I needed to buy a whole new wardrobe. The gynaecologist put me on some diet to gain some weight "as it was not proper for a breastfeeding mother to be this small" which made sense. The man did not believe his eyes when he finally pulled through to see his child. He was confronted by a sexy and energetic me than whatever else he might had been expecting. Oh boy, that's when my troubles began. He started being insecure, wanting to know my every movement from the moment I woke up until bedtime if he was not around. When around, he would constantly ask "where are you going" each time I stood up to go to the bathroom, kitchen, or bedroom and insisting on driving me everywhere I went. The church incident though was the final straw and relations had to be cut.

Obsession can lead to deadly consequences. Mine would have been decorated ears and lack of control over my life if he had continued to stick around after the mutilation. I now live for me and my daughter, no romantic entanglements for me in the foreseeable future. Take care my people and always be alert for those danger signs which might turn deadly if unattended to.

AN EMOTIONAL WRECK

Siphokazi stood transfixed outside the kitchen window willing herself to cry but tears would not come. She just could not cry for the witch and was mortified to actually feel her heart swell with satisfaction at the news. What kind of a daughter would find delight at the news of her mother's passing. She really required not just prayers but a weeklong intercession with the highest priest to exorcise whatever demons that possessed her. *No, it cannot be true that she is gone. Let me eavesdrop objectively.* She thought as the ramifications of her mom's possible death surfaced. There was no way she would leave her with that man and their six children. Was it not enough that she was already a mother figure to the family? For her mother to just leave her like that with the spiritual and emotional burden which was gonna be the ultimate cross to bear? No ways.

Siphokazi poked her head through the window to hear them properly whilst hoping that her dad or Aunt won't catch her eavesdropping. They had lowered their voices with her dad trying and failingly to calm his sister so he could get more information from her.

"Sisi please have some water to calm you down. I am battling to understand the words coming from your mouth. Take a deep breath and start from the beginning, slowly this time."

There was a pause and Siphokazi could imagine her aunt's adam's apple working furiously, odd thing that on a woman, and froglike eyes almost popping out of their sockets with that bird's beak of a mouth trying desperately to drink from the cup elegantly but failing miserably. She could determine by her father's impatient sighs that there was spillage all over the kitchen. She had never in her entire young life come across a sloppier individual than her aunt, poor soul.

"Ngiyaxolisa bhuti. Shock took over and I lost my mind a bit. What I am trying to say is that Sissy, my daughter, was hit by a car and the driver has apparently rushed her to the hospital."

A groan of disappointment rose like bitter bile from Siphokazi's insides, and it took every ounce of willpower to stop herself from screaming out loud.

She was unsure whether to laugh with relief or cry with disappointment at the unpalatable news that the witch was still alive. Shelving her unsavoury thoughts, she brought her reflections to the news of her cousin. Sissy was one of the few relatives from both paternal and maternal side that she genuinely liked and got along with. She edged closer to the window again to find out whether she would make it and even remembered to say a little prayer for her to survive the accident.

"Let me get my car keys and jacket sisi. Go wait for me outside, where the car is."

"Kulungile bhuti and thank you for everything. I would probably feel at ease once we reach the hospital and I have seen my baby and heard from the doctors the extent of her injuries."

Siphokazi hightailed to the toilet at the approaching footsteps and pretended to come out as her aunt turned the corner towards the back where her father's car was parked outside the yard.

"Sawubona Auntie, hoping all is well with you and family."

"Phila Siphokazi. All is well my child except for your cousin Sissy."

"Oh, what is wrong with her?" Feigning ignorance so cunningly.

"She was hit by a car on her way back from school…"

"Oh no Auntie! Is she alright?" That was an Oscar award moment, Siphokazi thought as she clapped her hands on her cheeks in shock.

"We pray so child. The months of July and August can be quite harsh, apparently a gust of wind blew up her dungaree as she was about to cross the main road and she missed seeing the car coming towards her at high speed." Aunt sighed sorrowfully. "From the information gathered at the scene is that it was a high impact hit, she flew into the air and landed with a thud on the tarmac---" An involuntary shudder passing through her aunt amidst tears pouring out. Siphokazi didn't know the right way of handling the situation and awkwardly stood there patting her aunt like she would a stray unwashed poodle.

"Sisi, are you coming or what?" Aunt Flo started at her brother's voice as if she had momentarily forgotten her surroundings. She moved in the direction of the car but seemed to change her mind and turned back to Siphokazi.

"Be good child and know that things will be okay one day. Don't lose hope." Siphokazi stood frozen unsure at the meaning of the words or the bear hug that followed the statement. Was Auntie aware of the current situation, did the adults discuss them and if so, why no one has ever intervened to ease the burden she was carrying? She disengaged from the hug and turned towards the kitchen, defeat and bitterness at the adult expectations and duties weighing heavily on her shoulders. She needed a good cry and a nap before the older kids got back from school. Thank goodness her father would not be around and for once she would have time to herself to think on the direction her life should take.

"All the best auntie, I will keep Sissy in my prayers." She thought to add before disappearing into the house. She heard rather than saw the car rev up and leave. She had on frequent occasion questioned her existence in the world and had several run-ins with the man above. If He indeed was a caring Father who loved all His children equally and could be everywhere in the world simultaneously why had He forsaken her.

At age sixteen she was already exhausted by life, and this had been on-going from the age of six when the first sibling came and had carried on to child number six. Her mom had applied and gotten a job at Doha as a nurse when Siphokazi turned seven and each visit back home came with either a pregnancy or delivery of a baby before she disappeared within three months of giving birth leaving the baby in the care of Siphokazi. Studying and taking care of the babies and the household became her birth right. She did everything she could at juggling these acts which became more and more onerous and a struggle as the kids grew older. She was required, forced would be the right word, to leave school at the age of fourteen because "she was old enough and could read and write" to take care of the family full-time.

The demands on her young body and soul had now moved from unpaid nanny and maid to possible sexual partner. The man of the house intimated a few months ago, when her boobs started growing, that she was now a woman and needed to fulfil all the needs of a functioning family that her mom was unable to meet being so far away from home. She had so far avoided any sexual contact as the last born was very demanding and deemed to suffer from autism. A mild form and spent most of her waking time with Siphokazi and at night she ensured that she was surrounded by the younger kids in her bedroom. She was unsure how long she could hold him off as she had seen the increased lust from him and was at a point where she feared some form of sexual attack soon on her person.

Siphokazi fell into a deep sleep she had not encountered in the past five years when the three last babies were born in succession of each other. She saw herself as a five-year-old dressed to the nines going to church with a fine young lady, but her face was obscured. There was love and admiration all round as they twirled in front of the mirror applauding their goods looks and beautiful clothing. The mirror did not lie as they undeniably looked smashing. After church they would go to Chicken Licken for lunch and finish the day off with movies at Ster Kinekor. Those were wonderful times. The scenario in her dream changes to a burnt taxi with people strewn all over the surrounding area whilst others remained trapped inside. The smell of burning flesh permeated the area and there was uncontrollable wailing as people combed through the debris. Paramedics arrived at the scene and declared the burn victims deceased "nothing further to be done except move them to a mortuary" and they focused their attention on those lying injured on the ground. Providing CPR and wheeling them to the ambulances waiting to transport them to hospitals.

Siphokazi grabs at the man in a white coat screaming "I want my mommy, where is my mommy" and he asks what her mommy looked like or was wearing so he could help her find her. A beautiful green dress with buttons in front and white high heels, a gap-toothed young Siphokazi tries her best to describe what her mom was wearing as she hopes that it would assist the man find her mom quicker. She is hungry, thirsty, and needs to sleep as it is way past her bedtime. The man searches frantically and comes back with a sombre face unsure how to break the news to a five-year-old. He comes back with an unknown woman who keeps screaming "I am sorry my baby, I am so sorry baby girl".

Siphokazi woke with a start and was shocked to hear the kids' voices in the lounge. She must have been really tired for her to not have heard the brood come in. The dream had been so vivid, and it revived snippets of her past life that confirmed that she was not part of this family. She needed to find the truth about her family and where she came from. She was going to sneak out later tonight to visit a friend who was good with technology to see if he could not help piece some of the puzzles for her through his advanced search expertise. It was time to reclaim her life and discover who she was outside this family. She had done and given all she could to them and needed to leave now before that man could bring additional misery in her life and possibly give her an unwanted baby as his seed seemed to germinate and multiply unashamedly.

"Hello kids, sorry I did not hear you come in. I will start the fire and get the food going." A contrite Siphokazi stated the obvious whilst hoping that the man may be delayed in the hospital and not catch her slacking. She did not want to raise unnecessary attention on herself tonight for her plan to work properly.

"Don't worry Siphokazi, we started the fire for you, and we will cook for you too if you guide us." Tshepiso, the eldest chimed in amongst the high levels of clatter from the young ones.

"Thank you Tshepiso for the offer. You can be my sous chef if you don't mind because things will move quicker that way." A beaming Siphokazi even offered the kids cookies as a treat for their conduct.

The man came later looking frazzled, ate his supper, took a bath and bade them farewell as he made his way to bed. Siphokazi, realising that there would never be an opportune time like that moment, ran to the outside toilet and set for a while with the door partially opened so she can observe the family's movement. She left the toilet five minutes later and headed towards the dustbin to retrieve a small overnight bag she had placed inside which contained essentials once certain that there was no one coming out. She scaled the wall using the side where she had earlier stacked a couple of bricks to help her jump over to the neighbour's side. She did not worry much about them as they slept with the "chickens". When she landed on their side all was quiet and dark as she had expected. She went over their low rickety fence and ran to her friend's car which was parked near the local sportsground.

"Hello skeem, thank you for doing this." Siphokazi panted as she settled herself in the front passenger seat.

"I will do anything for you skeem. I am flourishing because of you." Timmy saw the puzzled look on Siphokazi's face but left her hanging. There was so much to be done and she needed to leave this place ASAP before they discovered her missing. They had small chatter on useless stuff as they drove away before Timmy hit her with his findings.

"I decided to start with you, by focusing on your face using your old to current pictures, thanks to them because I hit a goldmine. I so wish we had done this earlier."

Siphokazi was almost falling off her seat with excitement, she knew Timmy was good but had not expected results this soon.

"Hit me with it, what did you find?"

"Well, the most amazing news is that your mom is still alive…"

"Of course, she is alive and leaving well in Doha…"

"No, not that one. I mean your maternal mother."

"What! Wait a second. What are you trying to tell me?"

"You were stolen Siphokazi. At the accident scene. The incident you told me about was real. It was not a dream. It happened."

Siphokazi could only stare at Timmy in shock. She was lost for words. She always knew that there was something amiss with her current situation but never fathomed it could be this deep and vile.

"Siphokazi, your mom did not die in the fire and has spent the last ten years looking for you. Only, she has been relying mostly on the police and you know how messed up that can be."

"How, where and what is the story with the current family?"

"This 'mom' used to be a paramedic before she joined the nursing profession and was one of the people who were at that accident scene."

"Wow---"

"Yes, and that is how you landed up with 'her family'." Siphokazi noted the tone around family but decided not to follow up on it yet as she had so many questions regarding her own family.

"She was not married at the time your paths crossed and she took you in and passed you on as her child to the future in-laws." Siphokazi took it all in, the ill-treatment and all the nonsense that came with that family now made sense.

"How come I could not remember any of this until this afternoon when I had that dream?"

"Severe trauma and conditioning can cause that."

"Still---" Something was not adding up for Siphokazi.

"We need to stop before I throw up, this is too much, man. Where did you find all this information? This was all too much for Siphokazi to handle. Not only had she discovered that these were not her parents as she had suspected at times but to learn that her mom was alive was way beyond comprehension.

"Where are you taking me?" Siphokazi asked as she finally took cognisance of their surroundings and realising that they were heading towards the freeway.

"To meet your birth mother…"

"Oh, don't you think we should have discussed this before you made that decision." Sighing heavily.

"You have just hit me with shocking news, and I need space to digest all that."

"You are absolutely correct Siphokazi. Please forgive me for allowing my excitement to take over common sense. Let me call her and re-arrange."

Huh, men like Timmy were sweet but this usually got accompanied by impulse. He looked crushed and Siphokazi understood that he was trying to help but just wished that he had waited to consult with her first. She needed to digest the information provided and prepare herself mentally and emotionally prior to meeting with her mother whom she didn't even know. Who was like a stranger to her. Huh.

"Can we stay over elsewhere? I have some money saved and can afford to book a cheap overnight stay and we can then visit her tomorrow once I am refreshed and have digested the news fully."

"Agreed, one night should not be a problem." Siphokazi watched Timmy as he made a call to her mom to re-arrange their visit and to apologise for the inconvenience.

"She understood, although she sounded a bit sad. Apparently, she had cooked all your 'favourite' foods that she acknowledges might no longer even be the case."

This sent them giggling as they realised that the tastebuds of a person changes as they grow older and certain food items like pumpkin, mash and custard might no longer have the same appeal at age sixteen.

Siphokazi asked Timmy to stop at a Chicken Licken outlet for a takeaway as nostalgia from days gone by hit home again. They found a Formula 1 hotel with room availability and decided to share a room to save costs as it came with bunk beds.

Siphokazi woke up to dozen messages and missed calls from home which ranged from concern to deranged depending on the caller. She ignored all of them and decided to be selfish for once and focus on her own life now that she knew part of her history. They had breakfast at Wimpy before heading to the suburbs of Walmer and were greeted by security at a gated community who asked for identification and address of the host.

They were let in with no hustles and Siphokazi felt her insides working and knew that nerves had taken over and prayed that she would not require a toilet upon arrival. She had always found it abnormal for people to travel from their homes without emptying their bladder or along their way and demand a toilet before even sitting down to greet and engage with their host. Thus, she wanted to avoid that at all costs and used the last few minutes down the lengthy driveway to their destination to meditate and calm her nerves. She felt Timmy's hand encircle hers and giving a quick squeeze before letting go and leaving her feeling more bereft.

"That's her. I would know and recognise that lady anywhere. She came to my dream looking exactly like that and wearing a similar looking dress. The perfume wafting through the window is all her…"

"You can smell from that far and are we going to leave the car anytime soon? She has been waiting for a while now---"

Timmy commented just as Siphokazi's mother left her spot and headed towards the passenger door, I guess she couldn't wait any longer. She reached the door just as Siphokazi was getting out and they collided into each other. There was no denying this person was her mom. The touch, the smell and tight squeeze was all her and more. They allowed their tears to flow unchecked as pain, emotions, loss, and physical distance that had separated them melted away. Siphokazi was home. She not only knew it but felt it.

"Welcome home my baby, how mama has missed and searched for you all these years. Thank you to your friend here for reaching out. Please come in, where are my manners."

Timmy followed closely behind them as her mom held to her tightly as if afraid that she might disappear from her sight again.

"I cooked all your favourite food yesterday and then realised that you had grown and might no longer like the same things, but you are going to eat them because as you might remember no one cooks like me." Timmy burst out laughing before adding "you might be surprised to find that no one cooks like Siphokazi, she might have inherited it from you".

"Oh, that's wonderful. We are going to have fun in the kitchen catching up and bonding through

144

delicious flavours. Please have a sit whilst I bring some snacks."

Siphokazi and Timmy could not help but be drawn towards a mental case filled with pictures of little Siphokazi with and without her mother. You could just see the motherly love and bond the two shared. It was puzzling to Siphokazi how she could have blocked all that out until yesterday and yet it was quite clear that she had a healthy relationship with her mom. Possibly the aftermath of the crash, the burnt victims and supposed loss of her mom had led to the mental block. She wondered how her life could have been like had she remembered all this before, never mind she was here now. Her phone rang just then, and she recognised the Doha number and knew immediately who was on the other line.

"Good day Mrs Mhlanga, Siphokazi speaking."

The voice on the other line came out sharp, loud, and furious and the phone was snatched from her hand before she could respond to the insults.

"Lalela la wena sela ndini! You are not going to talk like that to my daughter ever again and if I were I would look for a good lawyer because I am coming for you and your husband for abducting my daughter whilst I was fighting for my life…" Siphokazi could hear mom Mhlanga interjecting and making excuses about having thought that her mom would not make it and doing the best she could for the little girl, but her mom would have none of it.

"Leave all your explanations for the courts and if I were you, I would book my next flight home before you get deported. I don't think you would want to be embarrassed like that, a whole matron." Siphokazi's mom dropped the call before further engagement could ensue.

"That she-devil would get what's coming to her for the trauma and agony she has caused us. I lost a fiancé and a child at the same. The bastard could not stand my 'ugly burnt stomach' and I had no child to hold on to for comfort either. Yerrr, I have suffered."

Siphokazi went to hug and comfort her mother as the events of today and past ten years seemed to overwhelm her. It was decided that Siphokazi and Timmy would spend the night with her whilst they plotted on the best possible revenge on Mrs Mhlanga.

"Ladies, you might want to wait a bit on that. Those kids need to be re-united with their families first before anything happens to them."

"What do you mean? Those are Mrs Mhlanga's kids. I was there when she gave birth…"

"Did you actually see her at full-term or give birth?"

"Weeelll, no. She used to fly in directly to the hospital and come home with the baby or spend a few days with us before disappearing to the hospital."

"Exactly, I discovered yesterday that Mrs Mhlanga is part of a syndicate that steals babies at hospitals by informing parents that they gave birth to stillborn..."

"What, no Timmy? Are you saying all those kids do not belong to the Mhlangas?" Siphokazi asked with disbelief and wonder at what else Mrs Mhlanga was capable of.

"Most of the stolen kids are sold off but she kept you guys hoping that you can bring higher income later on when sold to prostitution. You only survived this long because the husband caught feelings for you."

"He knows?"

"He is the driver of the scam."

"But he was not there when I was brought home."

"He was in the picture even then."

"Amazing, I would not have figured that out because she has always brought home kids with similar features."

"Yah, she is good with profiling." Timmy concluded.

"You managed to source all this information in the two hours you had?"

"You know I am good."

Siphokazi mulled over this matter and realised that the kids' lives were more at risk than she had ever anticipated and that they needed to move very fast as Mrs Mhlanga knew they were onto her. She was happy that she had enlisted Timmy to help figure things out. It was now up to her mom and law enforcement to handle the matter to its conclusion. She had been abused and was an emotional wreck for so long that she knew that nothing, but her mother's nurturing and therapy would ease her back to normalcy.

Breaking news: A woman's chopped body was found stuffed in a suitcase bound for South Africa. It is alleged that she was part of a baby trafficking syndicate and had been on the list of Interpol's most wanted for a while now. It is suspected that she may have tried to outrun or swindle her partners leading to her demise. The husband who is also thought to have been part of the syndicate is on the run after receiving a tip-off. Members of the public are advised that he is armed and dangerous and should not attempt to apprehend him but rather inform the police when spotted.

Siphokazi and her mom re-winded the news with disbelief. They had met with a lawyer just yesterday to get the wheels of justice going in order to assist in getting the kids re-united with their families with the help of social workers. It seemed that the syndicate had decided to remove the weak link to protect their cover. Wow, what an end to years of criminality and trauma to affected families.

"Chicken Licken my baby?"

"I think that would be a fitting ending to this saga mom."

BATTLING IT OUT

W hat are you doing in my bedroom?" Vela freezes and Jabu goes tense next to him. Where did he come from? He is supposed to be out of town for the weekend, eish he will not hear the end of it from Jabu. He is forever accusing him of impulsiveness and never stopping to assess a situation before jumping in with his long feet.

He turns to confront the individual and to defend himself if need be. Only to face a very-dark man wearing a sangoma's cloth, red dreadlocks with beads, more beads around his throat with a small veal (probably containing animal gall or fat), white vest and barefooted. He cannot face Jabu who will most definitely have accusatory eyes. How was he to know that the target's house was owned by a sangoma, although this one seems to fit the bill of a witchdoctor than a healer judging by the raging fires burning in the depth of his soul, those eyes can stand on their own and tell stories.

"Speak, I haven't got the whole night to entertain criminals! I have clients waiting."

"We came to rob the house. We were informed that you have a safe stuffed with gold." Vela is shocked by Jabu's brazenness. Who confesses to a possible crime, not that there is any other truth given that the man caught them righthanded as they were tampering with the safe's locker, using his brother's brilliant wizardry on matters requiring hacking systems or breaking in.

"I see. I like your style. You are going to be quite useful to me. Wait here, I will be back shortly and don't try anything foolish like running away because you don't want to incur my wrath."

He goes to the corner of the bedroom to pick up a white cloth and leaves. Jabu gives him a deadly look but maintains his silence before flopping down on the carpeted floor, and Vela follows suit.

"Ngiyaxolisa ndoda, how was I supposed to know that we were attacking a sangoma's home?" That angry look again and nothingness. Vela needs to get to him before the man returns.

"Look I wanted to get to the safe first before those idiots. I am tired of our current situation of hand-to-mouth existence. I need to create a better life for us."

151

"Your problem is that you don't think and plan before you act. Had you done your homework you will have gathered useful information about your target or rather had you considered sharing the details, I will have done the research for you. Mxm!"

Jabu turns his back to look the other way and Vela knows that he has lost him. The door opens and in comes the man of the homestead.

"Follow me to the rondavel. I don't conduct business inside my house." They sheepishly follow him to one of the rondavels on the far side of the massive yard. He hesitates slightly at the door before beckoning them to take off their shoes and come through. They are shown to the "men's" side of the room and required to sit on the grass mat provided. The man squats in the middle of the room and starts mumbling to himself which slowly increases to a roar. He is hissing, spitting, and summoning his ancestors calling them by their clan names of Mvelase. The room is covered with smoke from the woodfire burning at the corner and the incense from the enamel plate in front of Mvelase. He throws the bones and pokes whilst chanting. He gives Jabu furtive looks with each poke until Jabu starts fidgeting nervously next to Vela. Vela's palms are sweaty as he hopes and prays that nothing bad will befall Jabu. How will he explain his brother's disappearance to their mother?

"You are going to fulfil my mission." Mvelase states with a self-satisfied smile. His eyes still on Jabu.

"Yes, you are the one---"

"What are you talking about? I'm tired of this nonsense. Punish us if you have to or let us go." Vela slaps Jabu's wrist, is he trying to get them killed or worse bewitched.

"I like your insolence. You are going to need it for where you are going, both of you actually." What is this man on about?

"Yes, I'm sending you boys to ancient Egypt. There is something I need there and only brave and fearless people like you can undertake this mission for me."

"Ancient Egypt no longer exists old man." Jabu laughs mirthlessly. Vela pinches him at the man's changing face. He doesn't want to die in some remote area. No one knows they are here. Even their gang whom Vela was going to double-cross. This robbery has been in planning for the past few months, and they were supposed to execute the plan next week. Vela fast-tracked things a little bit after they were provided with maps of the compound. He knew everything about this place, except that minor detail regarding Mvelase's occupation. The gang leader only mentioned that the man had unearthed a gold stash in the Drakensberg Mountains which was now kept safe in his bedroom. None of them were really paying attention to the other details about Mvelase or should Vela say he was not interested in anything else other than retrieving the riches. Look at them now, stuck in a lion's den.

"That is why I will be sending you back in time. I want Pharaoh Ramses II's head and you two are going to deliver it to me."

"The herbs must have gone to your head old man. There is no black man who possesses such powers, otherwise we will not still be suffering."

"Your suffering has nothing to do with me but with whom you have entrusted with your lives and voting power." Mvelase states disgustedly. "You are toothless, laughing at 'Karens' but behaving worse than them. Always whining and moaning whilst waiting for someone to save you. Pitiful!" He leaves the rondavel in a huff, probably to cool down. Vela is unsure of what has possessed Jabu, but his conduct is worrisome.

"What is wrong with you? Why are you provoking the medicine man?" Vela whispers furiously.

"He is delusional. It must be addressed before he turns us into zombies or flying witches." Shrugging dispassionately.

"I have changed my mind. You leave tonight. I will place you there just before the plagues attack Egypt. You must be in the thick of things and as close to Pharaoh as possible." Oh, he is back and calm.

"What is the plan?" Why is Jabu entertaining this mumbo jumbo.

"You boys are either quite smart or very dumb. We shall find out soon which it is. No one has ever attempted to break-in and steal from me. They know me."

He beckons them to come closer and blow on the open pouch cradled in his hands. He smears a jelly ointment on their foreheads and makes small incisions inside their wrists before injecting herbs.

Vela almost howls in pain at the burning sensation it brings. He can't believe how putty they have become. The man is in command of their bodies and doing as he pleases.

"Swallow these herbs. They will help you hear and understand the old Arabic language. You are a fast learner and might even be able to converse in the language." Pointing at Jabu. "This a powerful herb, swallow everything if you want." He picks another vial and orders them to pack it in their rucksack, apparently this will bring them back once the mission is executed.

"How you carry out the mission is up to you. Just bring me that head."

"Why? What is important about it?"

"I am losing my powers. There are all these miracle prophets sprouting all over the place. I have been advised to get the head of the most powerful leader to have ever lived and this guy is it. He faced the big man and fought against him to the bitter end." Stating gleefully.

"That takes bravery. You are not on the same level, but you might just surprise me again." Vela cannot understand why he can't do the job himself. Concluding that he is a coward and needs sacrificial lambs.

They are given another concoction to drink and find themselves transported to an era of vast terrain where stars are brighter, and your gaze can travel far. They find a donkey tied to a branch in the middle of the desert and know that it can only be from Mvelase. It's probably here to spy on them muses Vela.

They untie the donkey but are unsure of what to do with it. They are city boys and have never ridden a donkey or even a horse before. All they know is Uber and Taxis. Jabu says that they should attempt to climb on top and it starts moving of its own accord once they are settled. It seems to know the way. Vela looks at the sky and is mesmerised by it. The moon and stars illuminate their journey way better than streetlights. He can actually breath fresh air without sneezing with allergies caused by smog.

In the early hours of the morning, they come across a group of shepherds who seem completely confused by their attire and appearance. Jabu shakes his head in anger, confused as to why none of them had factored that in their banishment to a time captured in history books.

"Who are you and where do you come from?" A nineteen-year-old looking boy ventures to ask. Vela shrugs in response. The language is understandable, but he cannot formulate a response.

"We are from the future. We have been sent to warn the King about the impending disaster." Jabu states clearly and assuredly. Vela is confused by his response. How do you tell strangers such things and how did he manage to communicate so well with them? Their kinky hair, dark skin and branded clothing topped with bucket hats are definitely out of place. He reckons that maybe only the truth can indeed spare their lives.

The boys are circling them in wonder and shock that they can understand them.

"What are you talking about?" The boy hits them with a follow-up question. He must the leader of the crew, concludes Vela.

"The God of Moses is very angry with the King and wants to punish him unless he…"

What is wrong with these boys, why are they laughing at such a serious matter?

"Moses, the stuttering man who ran away from the old King. We know of him and how he was discovered, raised to live a pampered life before he turned against the hand that fed him." No wonder the old man could not be taken seriously if even the kids think he is a joke.

"Dude, this is gonna be harder than I thought." Vela confers with Jabu in isiZulu figuring it safer that way.

"Yeah, I can see that. We have to try though. I can't figure myself living like this. My bum is sore from riding this donkey and it has only been for one night." Yeah, Vela feel his pain because he is right there with him.

"You look strange, your language and dress sense is even stranger. You can't be seen by elders if you want to live long enough to find your way home." It is decided by the crew that they will spend time with them in the wilderness until they can figure their way back home. None of them is interested in getting them closer to the palace or at least the village.

"Listen, the God of Moses is going to bring suffering to the land of Egypt. Some of it will include the plague of blood, plague of frogs, plague of gnats and flies." Jabu tries hard to persuade the boys about the coming disasters, to no avail.

"Okay, can one of you go home and ask the elders to observe any changes in the coming days. That is all we ask you of."

"Well, Abasi and Babu are on their way back to pick up some suppliers for us. They will observe and report back." Stating with disbelief.

Vela and Jabu are provided with robes, food, and apportioned sleeping quarters. The following day they are given menial tasks to perform as a contribution towards their stay with the shepherds. Days and nights pass without a word from Abasi and Babu. Vela has seen the older boys whispering amongst themselves whilst looking in their direction.

"Bro, I am starting to worry. I think these ones are plotting something against us."

"Agreed, keep your eyes open at all times. We leave tonight…"

"What is that?" Vela notices a group of men heading their way on horseback led by Abasi and Babu in front who are pointing in their direction. They attempt to run for it but are quickly surrounded by the shepherds. They are outnumbered and stuck. Their donkey disappeared on the first day in the grazing site.

"Who are you?" A mean looking Egyptian barks out. He looks like he stepped out from a Gladiator movie bar the helmet and pteruges (defensive leather skirt).

"Jabu and Vela."

"Where are you from?"

"South Africa."

"Where is that? I have never heard of…"

"You are wasting time Mukarramma. You two come with us." They are scooped and thrown into different horses led by other giants. The contingent heads back in a hurry, leaving behind a swirl of dust. They didn't even have enough time to cover their heads with headscarves and as if becoming aware of the situation, the horses are abruptly brought to a halt, and they are covered before taking off again.

They reach the gates of the palace at dawn and are taken to the soldiers' quarters where they are quizzed throughout the night. They want to know who they are, what is their relationship with Moses and how do they know so much about the events taking place currently?

"Sir, as mentioned in the past twenty hours. We are from the future and have no relations with Moses." Vela is tired and his body is sore from the beatings. He is afraid to look at Jabu. He is too quiet for his liking. He is scared to check in case he has not made it. South African police can learn a thing or two from these guys. They don't play. The beatings from the sjambok have been brutal. His skin is torn and there is blood all over him and on the floor.

Mukarramma surveys them and seems to make up his mind about something. He orders that they be cleaned, wounds tended to and be given food. Everyone looks shocked but carry out the instructions. Vela checks on his brother who seems lost in his own world. He knows that look. Jabu is capable of shutting down and removing himself from pain and suffering. Be there physically but detach emotionally from whatever atrocities may be taking place. He wishes that he could be like that at times but knows that it is not within him. He wants to feel and deal with the pain at that instant and be done with it.

They are literally dragged to the well as their bodies have become numb with pain. They are tended to and smeared with oils to heal the skin. Vela knows that they won't sleep that night. The pain is excruciating. They spend the night alternating between their haunches and buttocks. He finally succumbs to sleep in the early hours induced to sleep by the herbs provided by one of the slaves carrying out all sorts of menial to hard labour chores in the palace.

"Up, up, up. This is not a hotel." Gosh, Mukarramma is back with another mean looking giant. This one was not present the day before.

"These are the young men I was telling you about." Mukarramma informs the giant.

"So, you say you are from the future, yes?" They nod simultaneously in too much pain to do anything else.

"How did you come to know about these plagues?"

"From the bible." Jabu mumbles after a long silence.

"A what?"

"A bible. It is like a scroll or hieroglyphs written for believers in God."

"The God of Israelites?"

"Yes, but through His son we have all been…"

"His who?"

"Son—" Jabu leaves the sentence hanging. It is clear that this aspect is way over their heads. Vela cannot wait to get back home and deal with that Mvelase. He is certain that he has not done anything to improve his security system and can be accessed easily. It is taboo to kill a sangoma but this time he is prepared to test the gods and live with the consequences. Why would anyone want to strengthen themselves with a head of a lunatic because those are the symptoms this Pharaoh guy is exhibiting? Why expose your people to such suffering when you can just order them to look after themselves by ploughing their own fields instead of relying on slaves. This situation brings memories of his home country where people work for pittance and are pitted against each other for meagre wages. Huh, such is life.

"All you need to know is that there is still the plague on livestock, of boils, hail, locusts, and darkness coming. Each one will bring more devastation than the other." Jabu says before passing out, possibly from pain. He leaves them looking at Vela who cannot help them out as he has not managed to speak the language. He shrugs and attends to his brother. More herbs are brought in to relieve the pain and revive Jabu as they realise that Vela is of no use to them given the communication barrier.

They are given clean robes and taken to the palace where Pharaoh and his officials are conferring with Moses and Aaron. Vela stands there in awe. He wishes he had access to a smartphone; gosh he can imagine how his tick tock account was gonna blow up from this footage. Although, it might be a good thing that he does not have access to it. Who will believe this stuff? He is sure that they will send him to Weskoppies for mental observation within a blink of an eye. Nah, this one is for the books to be released during his great-great-great grandchildren's era all digitised by Jabu of course. He notes Jabu from the corner of his eye taking pictures and videos without a care of the consequences. No one is paying attention to them yet, so he reckons it is okay. Jabu stops as soon as Pharaoh becomes aware of their presence.

"What is this Mukarramma? Who are these people?" He speaks so softly that Vela is taken aback but suspects that therein lies danger within that softness.

"Visitors from the future, Sir." Jabu and Vela squirm from the scrutiny.

"They know everything about his plans." Pointing at Moses.

"Oh, you brought more assistance to try and convince me of this idiocy. You are failing your God Moses." Turning to them, he instructs that they talk.

Jabu gets straight to the point. He seems to have been revived and to no longer care about the penalties. He mentions all the plagues that have passed and the upcoming ones leaving Moses and Aaron standing there gobsmacked. Vela wonders what the God of Moses will do to Jabu for playing out all his cards like this. There is no room to persuade Pharaoh now except to implement the ONE.

"Oh, your majesty. There is a big one. A finale you might call it. That one will be revealed by Moses when the time is right." He passes out. Vela is starting to suspect that these episodes might be self-imposed, or the man upstairs has decided to shut him up before he messes up with his plans completely.

Moses and Aaron with their entourage bid Pharaoh farewell and take leave having been usurped by these young visitors. Jabu and Vela are banished to their compound to stay in until it is decided what to do with them.

"Bro, wake up." Vela begs and screams to no avail. Jabu is definitely out and gone for a while. Vela bargains and pleads, promising that from hereon he will adhere to the rule of law and that "I will go back to varsity and finish my archaeology studies and you can pursue your hospitality ambitions." He wishes he had not dragged his brother down this rabbit hole and look at them now. Frozen in time with possibly no way of going back home without the King's skull. That lazy old man, using kids to carry out his evil ways. What a coward!

"Who are you talking to?"

"Thank God. You are finally awake. You had me worried there for a while."

"The beatings were harsh. My body collapsed from the inflicted pain." Jabu grimaces as he attempts to stand up.

"I know and I am sorry for doing this to you."

"Nah, it is all on me for not being strong and assertive enough. I am not doing this nonsense anymore if we get out of here. You are on your own now bro. I am tired of this life." The fatigue is there to see. Vela's heart aches for Jabu who has had to endure so much at the expense of his own life to achieve his big brother's wishes.

"I understand…"

Days turn into weeks, and they are eventually allowed to leave their quarters and roam about for limited periods. The land has been ravaged and Pharaoh is still holding on. Jabu gets restless on the eve of the plague of darkness and cannot seem to settle.

"What is wrong with you tonight. You seemed to have adjusted to this life, so what is this?"

"You remember what is coming after this right?" Vela raises questioning eyes. He is never good at memorising bible stories or anything much for that matter except when it comes to his favourite subject, archaeology.

"The plague of the firstborns is coming and that will be our cue to take the man out. I still have not figured out how we are going to do that because he is forever heavily guarded."

Vela gets him loud and clear now. They may be stuck in this life forever if they don't manage to behead the King by then. Just then Mukarramma summonses them to the King's palace. They find Pharaoh waiting with some of his guards.

"Everything you stated has come true. What is next?" Vela and Jabu exchange a nervous look.

"Speak now!"

"Death of all Egyptian firstborn sons and your skull as a finale."

"What?"

"Yes, your majesty."

"Is that what he wants? Is everything that has happened leading to that?"

"Yes, if you don't release the Israelites."

"That is not going to happen."

"How are you going to stop it? Everything foretold has transpired so far."

"What now?" Heaving uncertainly.

"Comply or re-write history."

"Re-write history, how?"

"You can change the narrative to preserve your land and its people with the help of the man who sent us."

"What does he want?"

"Power and a place in history books."

"Is this possible?"

"Anything is possible where we come from. We are here as proof of that." Jabu exploiting the moment.

"And my palace?"

"There won't be much left after your army drowns in the red sea pursuing the Israelites." Vela is amazed by his brother.

"How long do I have?"

"Six days before doom strikes."

"How do I get there?"

"We can take you with us. You can bring two of your guards. That is all we can manage to transport."

Pharaoh agrees, figuring that it might be his only chance to reverse the tragedies and save his kingdom.

That is how the boys delivered Pharaoh to Mvelase and left with his gold whilst he battled it out with the Egyptians to die at their hands or become the most powerful man on earth.

WON'T LET YOU

Darcy looked at the regal and composed figure of her mother manning the hallway and was amazed at its effect even now. She squared her fresh shoulders and followed her siblings into the study where the lawyer and their father waited. Her mother's clothes were lined up in rows, as if in a store boutique, on the far corner of the study. She spied *thee* coat and lunged for it uncaringly as to what the others would say.

"Darcy!" She ignored her father this time and stood admiring the mid-length mink jacket which had cost a small fortune, money that should have gone towards her college registration fee. She swallowed the bitter vile that had foamed at that memory which had caused a major rift between her and the family. This was her moment to own that one piece of item which their mother had deemed more important than sacrificing that money towards her studies, when funds were running low. Their relationship had never been normal. Always being critiqued for being sloppy, slow, lazy and not smart enough compared to her older siblings. Strange to be honest as in most families last born kids tend to be the most favoured and spoilt as parents would be tired or had learnt what works in this parenting business.

She tried it on and was encouraged as her thickish arms slid into the jacket without too much hustle. She was feeling good but was stopped in her tracks on her way to the nearest bathroom by her sister's sniggering comment "take that jacket off Darcy it's tearing. Shame man, she won't let you have it even in death! Haha…"

"Mandy, stop it. Darcy take the jacket off and come sit. I don't have all day. I must leave in the next two hours."

Both Darcy and Mandy looked at their father in surprise. Where was he rushing to? The woman was laid to rest only yesterday. Couldn't he at least pretend to be mourning her death for at least a week? They quietly joined their two older brothers in the couch and sat facing the lawyer who had assumed the only chair in the room whilst their father perched himself on the edge of the study desk. The room smelled of cigar and there was a whiskey decanter lying on the desk next to a used glass. Darcy wrinkled her nose at the unwelcome odour in the

173

room and she could tell that her father had spent most of the night in the study drinking the last remnants of the past twenty-eight years married to their mother.

"Good morning, all. This is rather unusual as you know that the unwinding of estates usually takes longer and is discussed a bit later after death or burial, especially when there are lots of parties involved." Mr Clive exhaled briefly as if the task at hand weighed heavier than anticipated. "However, your father requested this meeting before his departure. As you may or may not be aware he is flying out to Amsterdam in four hours."

Gasps and shock reverberated throughout the tiny study indicating that none of the kids had been briefed about this development. Mr Clive sought direction from Mr Lindela who just sat there strumming his fingers against his left thigh. Indications were that he wanted this matter concluded as quickly as possible so he could set-off.

"This is the last will and testament of Mrs Lindela as drafted by Clive, Manneli and Mdluli and witnessed by Ms Ngobela and Mr Small." There are bequeaths to staff and family members who were favoured by their mother. A sum of money to be donated to her church and an NPO she supported financially and was a board member of.

"To my darling husband Mthunzi our love proved stronger than all the tests that were thrown our way. May you find joy as you embark on the next chapter of your life." Mr Clive turned the page and looked at us. Surely, that cannot be it. After all the years they spent together building a life and legacy.

"To my sons I bequeath the family businesses to continue running them for you and your families including the next generation." Utter shock, Darcy and Mandy are absolutely horrified. They had thought the businesses would be shared amongst the siblings and their father. What in the name of horror and limited thinking was this. Their future kids would be left penniless whilst their brothers and families blossom, as if they have not benefited immensely already from assisting the parents in manning the businesses.

"Don't worry sisters, we will ensure that you also benefit from the profits as it has been the case prior." David deemed it necessary to budge in and soothe the boiling situation. Their father was still sitting there aloof as if all this had nothing to do with him.

"Mandy, I bequeath to you the summer house, its contents and the offshore investment which was opened in your name at birth." Mandy was suitably impressed and quite chuffed by this gesture as she had no interest in the company businesses except the financial benefits. This would assist with injecting much-needed equity into her craft business.

"To Darcy my dear child. Very independent and know-it-all. Always debating, challenging and being rebellious for no reason. I loved you even though most times I may not have always shown it." Mr Clive took a shallow breath before turning that final stab. "I bequeath to you my mink coat and any other items you may desire from my cupboard." What?? "I know and understand the love-hate relationship you had with that coat. Take care of it, especially its inner pockets which are quite fragile." Darcy sat motionless as if turned into stone.

How could she do that to her? Even in death she was still mocking her and cruelly tormenting her. That coat caused a major rift between them which took years to mend. What made it worse was that South African winters tended to be mild and so the coat only came out once or twice a year that Darcy had once jokingly stated that "mother, you should let me auction that coat so I can raise funds for the next semester." It was always a mystery to her that she always had to raise funding for her studies with all the money they had. Her father was just there for the vibes as the purse strings were controlled by the matriarch. These were her businesses after all.

Her mother's stance was that the older siblings had it tough and that the expectation that they should go easy on Darcy as the lastborn was ridiculous.

"No one is going to serve you things on a platter. You must work for them. Businesses crash, people lose their jobs or health. I am empowering you and giving you tools to survive any storm that may come your way." This narrative didn't sit well with Darcy then and it was not making any sense even now. Brothers left with businesses and a sister with an investment created in her name and all she got was a mink coat. A mink coat! The irony of it all is that it was the first thing she had pounced on when entering this room. Yah, mother was a jokester even in death.

Darcy thanked Mr Clive, picked up her bag and bade everyone farewell. She was no longer interested in anything else and intended to fly back to Singapore where she was currently based working for an international company as a strategist.

"Please sit Ms Lindela. I am not done." Darcy couldn't be bothered by all this but decided to sit rather than cause a commotion.

"I bequeath the Drakensberg house and its contents for the use of my family. Darcy must run and look after it as well as ensure that it serves the whole family and future generation. The financial allocation will flow from one of the businesses."

Darcy exploded. This was the worst insult that woman could have thrown at her. It was one thing to be left with nothing except the coat, but this was the most ridiculous thing she had ever heard. Her intention had been to leave the country in a week's time, but things had changed. She was no longer inclined to spend a minute longer in this house and her country. Her brothers and sister would take care of business. She was done.

"Darcy!"

"Sorry father. I am done here or was there anything else that requires my attention Mr Clive?"

"No, Darcy. That was all. Just so we are all on the same page. The will must still be endorsed by the Magistrate Court and any disputes that may arise between now and then will be dealt with through that process."

"You can tell them that I have no intention of staying or running this household. That is my dispute. I also don't want some washed out coat that does not even fit me, for what? To have people like Mandy having fun at my expense!" Darcy had totally lost control and had tried but failed dismally to compose herself. She bade everyone farewell again and headed for the door.

"Don't forget the coat!"

"Darcy!" Everyone screamed in shock as Darcy's handbag hit the mark. She wished she had done this sooner. Mandy had always provoked her and made fun of her including her body weight struggles. She made mean comments and never played the big sister role. Her brothers, although way older, had always been her best line of defence against school bullies and at home when the situation with her sister got too much.

She decided to leave with the coat just for the fun of it. She picked her bag and the coat on her way out. She went to her room and was glad that she had not bothered to unpack when she arrived on Wednesday. The only things worth packing were her toiletry bag and the pyjamas. She went online to see if she could update her flight details and find something leaving today. She was willing to travel and spend a night at the airport if needed be until something else came out. Fortunately, there were still seats available on the Singapore airline leaving Durban later that evening. She confirmed and paid the required amount for the change of flight details before searching for a meter taxi to drive her there. Pity that the homestead was situated in the middle of the Drakensberg where e-hailing services were non-existent.

"Come in." She responded to a knock on the door and hoped it would not be Mandy coming to irritate her again because she was going to cause an injury now.

"Are you okay?" Her father asked as he entered cautiously. What was he afraid of, Darcy wondered.

"I am well. Just sorting out my ride to the airport."

"You can come with me if you are ready. I leave in the next ten minutes."

"Thank you. I am ready." Darcy jumped to finish packing and was unsure about what to do with the coat.

"You can carry that as it would come in handy in the plane seeing that you are on the evening flight."

Yeah, that's true. Planes tended to become freezers, especially at night. She was never sure what was worse between a movie house or a plane temperature which generally left her with sniffles and ice-cold fingers. She enjoyed them both bar the cold they inflicted on the human body.

They travelled in relative silence for most of the journey from Drakensberg to King Shaka International Airport. They had never had any commonalities between them and when they did try to converse it fizzled out quickly, sounding contrived and unnecessary.

"Your mother loved you."

"Hmmm." Darcy replied feeling compelled to respond.

"It is the truth. We love you. It is just that we came from very strict families and became too lax with your brothers and sister." Father's fatigued sigh was strange.

"We tried hard not to become our parents and ended up raising spoilt and ungrateful kids. When you came along, we were already weary and not expecting another child." That sigh again.

"We vowed to raise you differently and, unfortunately, in the process became too hard and too harsh. I hope you will forgive us for what we have done to you."

Darcy kept quiet as she was unsure as to how to respond to these declarations. Her life had indeed been harsh and severe to the extreme at times which resulted in her eating a lot to ease the hurt and pain she felt at the seemingly uncaring parents. She wished that the parents had allowed her to grow and be her own person before imposing their fears on her.

"That money and the businesses are not gonna last. I know that for a fact. You cannot be saddled with the upkeep of that house. It is not your responsibility. She never discussed that aspect with me. I will help you fight against that because you would not get a cent for its upkeep from those useless brothers of yours."

Darcy was mystified by this statement and that her father was leaving everything behind knowing full well that it was going to crumble. She wondered why God had chosen her mother's womb to bring her into this dysfunctional family, because that was what they sounded like. Shoo, she was never coming back. This was not a life and place for her. The fascinating thing as well was that she had shed some of the weight accumulated living in her parents' house as soon as she left home. The issue was never her but that repressive environment.

"Why did mother leave all those things with them then knowing the kind of people they are?" That aspect didn't make sense.

"She didn't want you involved in their fights and believe me it is going to happen when the money starts running out. Hence, I asked that I don't receive anything."

Darcy realised that her parents had set her siblings up for failure knowing full well their incapabilities. Who did that? Who built a multimillion business to only destroy it upon their death and her father just walking away from it all as if it meant nothing was also troubling? She was beginning to feel way better about the whole situation. Those vultures would have eaten her alive for any crumbs she would have benefited. The only reason Mandy had lost interest in the coat was because of the money coming through and that it had split. She could still not fathom how that had happened because she had only been a size bigger than her mom and the coat was her exact size. Quite strange to be honest.

They made it to the airport with time to spare and dropped the car at Budget rentals before proceeding to international departures for check-in. Her dad was flying to Amsterdam via Dubai, and she was flying direct to Singapore international airport. They checked in and spent time browsing for magazines at Exclusive Books before settling down for coffee. Her dad was the first to board and he seemed close to tears as he bade her goodbye which was so unlike him.

"Let's keep in touch and guard that coat with all you have." This coat of misery was starting to bug her.

Who cares about this old thing? Yes, it still looked good but what joy has it brought her.

A hug and a goodbye kiss on the cheek from the fathership was the most bizarre thing ever. They were known for many things and display of warmth was not one of them, especially in public. This would be one for the grandchildren's bedtime stories.

"Remember to empty its pockets when you get home before taking it to the cleaners." His parting shot as he joined the boarding queue.

There was that issue again about the pockets. Ahh well, she would attend to it when she got home. Her flight was called next and was uneventful. The coat her kept nice and warm and she could actually feel her mother's presence enveloping her throughout the journey. She found her cab waiting when she left the airport which took her to her sanctuary. She hung the coat and forgot about it as life carried on. Months later she got confirmation that her mother's will and testament had been settled and that an audit of her mother's content had been completed and there were some items that could not be accounted for. She shrugged and informed them that had nothing to do with her and did not affect her as she got nothing anyway. Her father kept in touch and one day, a few months after the audit, asked about the coat.

"Oh, I still need to have it dry-cleaned. I can't bring myself to wear it."

"Okay, just don't forget to check the pockets."

"Yes daddy." Yes, the relationship had improved to those levels.

A couple of years went by with little communication from the siblings who were living a high life which excluded Darcy and their father when out of the blue Darcy received a called from David.

"Morning brother. This is a surprise."

"Yes, well sorry for not checking up on you as often as an older sibling should."

"No worries, is everything okay?"

"No, that is why I am calling…"

"Is it about dad?"

"No, he is fine. That is not the reason for my call." Okay, Darcy decided to let him continue.

"We need to sell the family house."

"What? Why? Mother's will was quite clear on that score."

"We need the money."

"But you have businesses."

"They have gone under. We need money to inject cash on the last remaining one."

"How? You can't sell that house. It was mother's wish."

"Darcy, this was not a request. It was just a courtesy call. We have all met and agreed…"

"So, you guys decided on this without me?"

"It is not our fault that you ran away from your family and chose to live as a separate entity divorced from its own family."

"You of all people know why I left."

"Yes, something about parents not caring and always acting like the victim. Get over it! Book yourself on the next available flight and come over here. Your

187

consent is also needed to sell the house and I hope you won't drag the matter." Before slamming the phone on her.

"Daddy, they want to sell the house."

"Let them." Huh, was he drunk? What was this?

"But daddy?"

"Let them be child. You will be fine. I take it you have not worn or checked that coat yet." Darcy kept quiet, embarrassed to admit that she had not found it in her for the past two years to wear the coat.

"Give them that consent and do something about that coat before moths destroy it."

"Yes, daddy." Darcy agreed, feeling defeated.

She fetched the coat from the loft storage when she got home and was mesmerised by its beauty. She had never taken time to admire it because of what it represented before. She decided to take it to the dry cleaners in the morning on her way to work so she could wear it. She checked and emptied its pockets as advised. There was a sewn inlet which she set about opening up with a needle. She found a pouch containing gold and diamond jewellery worth a fortune and almost collapsed with shock. She wondered how it was possible that these items were not detected at both airports, especially Singapore. She was trembling as she realised how much trouble she could have found herself in for failing to declare these items had they been detected then.

Out came a neatly folded letter in one of the pockets addressed to her in her mother's writing.

"Dear Darcy, if you are reading this letter, it will mean that we have finally reached that stage. I did this hoping that you would one day be tempted or that your father would push you enough to the point where you would be compelled to empty the coats pockets.

Your father and I did poorly in raising your siblings and we could tell early on the type of adults they were going to become. When you came along it forced us to act in a certain way so that you could not become targeted. I am happy that you were resilient in the face of hostility and the ruthless drive I threw your way. I knew my days on earth were numbered but bargained with God to keep me longer for your sake until you were old enough to stand on your own two feet.

I have provided well for you. You will never suffer as long as you live provided the resilience and attitude you showed from an early age prevails. I stashed money in offshore accounts and created investments vehicles under your name. I couldn't risk exposing your assets to your siblings as by now you would have been penniless. They would have used any means possible to take it from you or demand a share."

All this is yours to use as you wish and don't worry about your father. We made sure that he was well-taken off before my demise. Hence, you and your dad were not part of that Will and Testament. Let the vultures feast and enjoy what is yours in peace and let them be if they fight for the house.

I was pleased when you chose to move away from your country of birth and went to Asia to carve your own niche. They would never bother you there. I love you very much and I am sorry I was never gentle or warm towards you as a mother should be to her last-born child and yet it was necessary for them to believe that I didn't care much for you. You are the last person they will come for if they run out or find valuable items missing. Other items have been stored securely at mi-storage and the code is the last six digits of your ID number.

Keep well my child and take care. Mommy and daddy love you lots. Just remember that everything done was to protect you and I hope that you will find it in you to forgive me one day. Be good."

Darcy could not believe what she was reading. Her parents were real crooks because truly who does that. Things started to make sense because much as she had to raise registration funds or pay her way with regards to certain things, there was always some money deposited into her school account or bank account. It was not a lot to raise suspicions but just enough when she needed something or ran low. She was still a little hurt by the deception which was understandable but was also grateful that they had instilled hard work and ethics in her early-on. She had learnt that you work for things in life and that soft life was not a must just because you were born on the right tracks of the railway line.

The adage that caring mothers won't let you starve or go through lack whilst alive finally rang true. She was raised to persevere and be resilient no matter what. A kid from a wealthy family who did not thrive on handouts.

"Thanks to you and mom, now I understand everything. It hurts though." Having placed a call to her father.

"Don't hate us too much." Her father stated softly still unsure.

"It would take time for things to settle but know that it would be well. Love you." Darcy articulated and was startled to realise that she had never professed a love for her parents before.

"Love you too. Be good child."

Ahh, all is well.

EVIL LIVES WITHIN HER

Y ou are starting at the clinic tomorrow before you go to school."

I raise confused eyes before dropping my head quickly. I am never allowed to ask or question anything adults say, especially my mom.

"You must be ready to leave at seven AM sharp. Mrs Mngomezulu will accompany you." She concludes with no further explanations.

With a pounding heart I itch to ask the reason for the visit. There is nothing wrong with me. In fact, I can't recall ever requiring health services in the time I have been on this earth. Mrs Mngomezulu, our neighbour, hates me with passion and cannot even hide it. I have seen the way she looks at me, like I am a piece of baggage that needs recycling. She once threw a dead rat in my direction and laughed as if it was the most tickling thing to have ever happened. My observation has been that she does not like my whole family including Ma here, so her taking me to the clinic is a disturbing occurrence.

How I wish papa was here and not working nightshift. I have a tiny suspicion that mom timed this occasion so that there will not be a need to explain herself to him. I look around the kitchen trying to wreck my brain on how I can get out of this dilemma. I don't want to travel anywhere with that woman. Who knows what she will do to me at that clinic. *She is a qualified sister for goodness' sake and can't jeopardise her job.*

I finish eating and take our dishes to the sink to wash them before I call it a night. Being an only child has many drawbacks, part of it being that all the attention is on you. You cannot falter or cause mischief as there will be no one else to blame or cover for you. I bid mama goodnight, pick up the paraffin lamp and light it up before heading to my room.

Mama is long gone by the time I wake up. The coal stove is still going strong and there is boiling water at the edge of the stove for my bath. I fetch the bath basin, half fill it with cold water before topping it up with hot water, feeling the level of heat with my elbow each time I top up. I make porridge for breakfast and a peanut butter sandwich for school lunch. I am done with my morning when I spy Mrs Mngomezulu coming out of her house and I grab my schoolbag quickly and lock up. I don't want any comebacks later, like her complaining that I made her late for work.

"Morning Ma." I greet respectfully with head bowed.

She grunts and starts walking quite fast.

"You young girls think you are grownups." I have no idea what she is talking about, so I keep quiet.

She looks as if she is expecting a response, but I have none and this seems to irritate her more. The evil eye is out in full force. She is not even trying to hide it now.

"Look at you heading to the clinic instead of going to school. Your mother is doing a good thing at least. Others should learn from her and do the same before it is too late." I am lost and I should probably ask what is she referring to and risk being reported for insolence but instead I remain silent.

We walk to Mqantsa Section where her clinic is situated and find two nurses already setting-up for the day.

"Good morning sister." They greet in unison.

"Morning girls. Nurse Ngidi, please stop what you are doing and assist this girl. She must still go to school when we are done here."

"What is she in for Sister?" A puzzled Nurse Ngidi asks. It is not surprising as I am not showing any symptoms of sickness. I also crane my neck surreptitiously towards Mrs Mngomezulu's direction in anticipation of her response as I will finally hear the reason for the visit.

"Contraception." She says abruptly.

"What?" Both nurses sound as shocked as I am. I don't believe this.

"How old are you nana?" A slightly recovered Nurse Ngidi asks.

"Sixteen Nurse."

"Oh. You look much younger. Who sent you?"

"Her mother." Mrs Mngomezulu's tone ends the discussion.

Nurse Ngidi strides silently to pull out a clean file and fills in my details. Both nurses keep looking at me sorrowfully without saying anything. I am under Mrs Mngomezulu's care as per mom's instructions and they seem afraid to defy their superior or engage any further on the issue.

"Hurry up. The child must still go to school."

I am taken to a cubicle in an adjacent room where Nurse Ngidi prepares the injection.

"Give her Depo-Provera." Mrs Mngomezulu shouts from reception and the gasps from the nurses inform me that there is something seriously wrong with that statement. I look at the partially closed door and my instincts inform me to run from the place as quickly as possible. Something sinister is lurking in the clinic's rafters.

"I am coming back dear." She states as she puts down the prepared needle and joins the others at front office.

"Sister, we can't give her the Depo-Provera, she is young."

"Are you defying my instructions Nurse Ngidi."

"No Sister. It is just that we all know that we cannot administer Depo-Provera to children. It is not recommended."

"It is her mother's wishes. There is nothing we can do about it…" She responds begrudgingly.

"Her mother? Does she understand how these things work?" The other nurse asks incredulously. This whole thing does not make sense. Why would mother think I need contraceptives to begin with? I don't even have a boyfriend or have any interest in boys. I find them stupid and silly. Most of the guys in my class seem quite slow, you have to repeat things three times before they grasp any concept except of course on topics that involve girls. That is the only thing that gets them excited, even then the discussions are shallow. It is always about who is kissing or sleeping with who and what girl they think tastes better than others. I am not going to date fools who are going to discuss our private lives at school and whether I can kiss properly or not. I will rather be known as that proud virgin. This is an ultimate betrayal by my mother.

The whole township knows the type of girls that visit clinics. I am hoping that this will not raise any suspicions seeing that I came with Mrs Mngomezulu. I can't be too sure that she has not discussed this trip with her girls. My name is going to be tarnished and for what. Thank you, Ma, I say silently as I brace myself of what is to come. I am going to be labelled loose and every boy who avoided me like a plague will be chasing me from here on thinking I am now fair game. A tear rolls down my cheek and I do nothing about it.

What is worse is the conversation between the health workers indicating that I am also going to be given an incorrect contraceptive for my age. What did I do to mom to deserve this? I have tried everything in my power to follow her instructions and be a good child. I don't even have friends in our street. Maggie, my schoolmate who shares the same desk with me, is my only friend. We have a lot in common and can spend hours chatting just about anything from our parents, religion, state of the economy, fashion, and politics. Most of our peers in class cannot keep up with us, not only are we smart but we read a lot. I guess it comes from being only children and not being allowed to interact with other kids outside school premises.

"Look, I am following instructions. Do as I say and let the child go." Mrs Mngomezulu is done talking and clarifying now. Nurse Ngidi comes back and prepares a different injection. That can't be for human beings. It is thicker and longer, surely---

"Relax. You don't want the injection to break whilst inside your bum."

"Sorry nurse. It just that it looks scary. Like it should be used on a donkey's ass or something." I am not sure where that came from, but it relieves the tension I am feeling. Especially when Nurse Ngidi bursts out laughing and having to stop what she is doing to contain herself.

"What is going on there?"

"Nothing Sister, we are done." She gives me a clinic card and informs me that I must come back in three months' time for my next injection. I thank her and leave without saying anything to Mrs Mngomezulu. She was adamant that this was mom's doing when questioned by the two nurses who were not understanding why she did not offer proper advice to mom as the informed healthcare person. It is all puzzling to be honest. I have no time to spare and analyse the matter further. I walk to the main road to catch a taxi to school. I think I will make it for assembly looking at the time. I need to visit the library during break to read up on contraceptives. This is that one topic that Maggie and I have not entertained. We still see ourselves as kids and have no interest in any sexual activities. Otherwise, I will have researched and been better prepared for today. It is a pity that I was not informed in advanced about this trip or I will have made means to read up. Those nurses were freaked out and there must be a reason for their reaction. I suspect that my system has been poisoned and this thing is going to show itself in ways that will have long lasting repercussions.

I get off the taxi just as the school bell rings. There are still a few other kids loitering outside or getting off taxis and we all rush in before they close the gates. You don't want to be caught late in this school. Corporal punishment is the order of the day. You get beaten just for being a kid caught walking in the corridors regardless of the fact that you might be running an errand for a teacher. Kids are seen but not heard.

"You are late." Maggie states accusingly as we run towards assembly.

"Sorry." What is her problem? She is giving me an accusing look.

"You forgot about me, right?" She whispers as we join in singing the chosen hymn which happens to be one of my favourites, Guide Me O Thou Great Jehovah, I really need His guidance today.

"What are you on about?" Careful not to be caught chatting by the teachers.

"Maths!" Eish---

"Let us pray." Teacher Mpanza guides us in a short prayer before we disperse to our classes. I have Physics and Maggie has Accounting for her first period.

"Here, take my book. You will copy the assignment during our Zulu class. I will explain the concepts during lunch."

She takes the book as we move to our different classes. I am not sure if I will be able to share my experience with her. I feel sullied and violated. It is like my innocence has been taken away from me. Maggie and I have been looking forward to attending the reed dance when we turn seventeen which will be

202

our matric year and we thought it will serve as a form of matric dance outing for us. We follow all Zulu rituals within our limited spaces and the reed dance was our ultimate goal in preparation for our eighteenth birthdays when will be in university. I am still a virgin but somehow it no longer feels right to pursue that route. I am still a child and yet it is like I have been thrown into adulthood unexpectedly. I am not sure that I can ever view my body with the same innocence. What a life.

The day goes by uneventfully and finally it is home time. I am not sure how I am going to relate with my mom. I am angry and disturbed by what she has done. I am unsure why she would not discuss such a serious matter with me. The information I pulled on this Depo-Provera from the library is unsettling, especially the side effects that may come with it.

"You are too quiet."

"Sorry Maggie, I have a lot on my plate." I wave goodbye as I climb on a taxi and leave her standing there. Her home is a few streets away from school. She does not worry about transportation and her only challenge is time management, she is forever competing with the school bell to see who will arrive or ring first. Shame.

I do my daily house chores as soon as I get home before settling down to do my school homework. I see Mrs Mngomezulu in her yard. She keeps staring our way. I stay hidden from her sight in such a way that I can observe her through the doorway but not be seen. There is a self-satisfied smile on her face. She is really pleased about something.

I pick up the dishcloths and go to the laundry line to hang them up. Our eyes clash and her smile diminishes as my face and eyes tell her I know what she and mom did. They need to be reported for messing up a child's life like that and for what. The motive is still unclear just like the hate. I go back inside to finish my homework without exchanging a word. Mom comes back from work late in the evening and I find that I have nothing to say to her after the greetings.

"How did it go?" I stare at her and stay mute. I am wondering as to why she is not having this discussion with her new friend.

"I am talking to you."

"I don't know." Shrugging my shoulders in defiance. Dad comes in at that moment. You can cut the tension with a machete, that is how thick it is. He is off tonight so mom is cooking one of those scrumptious meals for her hubby.

"What is going on?" He is looking at mom.

"Nothing, I was just asking about her school day." Smooth mama, smooth. I see what she has done, expertly shifting the whole thing my way.

"Ntombi, what is happening?"

"All is well daddy, all is well." He throws the newspapers at me which means there is a must-read story or stories that he wants us to nibble on later after supper. I go to my room and start reading. The events of the day are soon forgotten as I learn that Nelson Mandela's release date has been confirmed for 11 February 1990. How did I miss it? Then I remember that the staunch activists were not at school today, they are probably going to drop off from school in preparation of that day. Dear Lord war is coming.

They have been prepping us for this day forever. They are going to join the underground operatives to reclaim the land by force. They have been waiting for the old man to come out and issue the directive. I wonder if there is any need to go back to school tomorrow or rather just wait for his release and join the struggle. I have been taught on how to handle and assemble a gun. I can shoot and prepare a petrol bomb in seconds as long as I have the tools. This is it. The moment we have been trained and preparing for.

I join my father and we plot until the wee hours of the morning. He advises me to go to school so that we don't raise any suspicions. No one knows about his underground operations except us. He does not share most of our dealings with mom because she scares easily and is not a good liar. We have always known that she will be the first to crack if the cops ever came sniffing around. I don't tell him about the clinic visit. The moment is not right. Weeks pass and the man comes out looking old and frail. We catch the live reporting on television. We wait with bated breath for that moment where he will rouse us to pick our guns and fight, instead he stands in the podium preaching reconciliation and urges us to go back to school and drop our weapons. We are stunned and unsure of ourselves.

There is confusion all over and I see people leaving the stadium where the event is being held. My dad goes to the toilet to re-group I reckon, leaving me wondering about the future. Dad comes back and starts a light conversation with us when he unexpectedly asks mom.

"What is happening with our daughter?" Things become tense and serious immediately.

"What do you mean love?" Mom asks innocently.

"Look at her, you can't tell me you have not noticed the changes in this child."

Thank goodness someone is verbalising the changes I have been observing in my body. My breasts have become huge and full, my tummy is bloated and protruding, and I have been bleeding continuously for weeks without ceasing. Neighbours have been giving me uncomfortable stares. I know they have been talking about me behind my back, although no one has said anything to my face yet. My school uniform is becoming tighter, and I may have to buy a bigger size soon if things don't change.

My dad is still waiting for an answer with ma looking everywhere but him. He shifts his gaze towards me and all I do is shrug and glance at mom. This is her gig. She mumbles something and stands up to clear the dishes. Odd, that has been my duty from the age of eleven.

I follow her to the kitchen where I fill up the washing basin with warm water and grab sunlight soap…

"Leave them. I will wash the dishes tonight. You need a break." Since when, I would like to ask but decide to let it go.

"You don't have to go back to the clinic ever again." Okay, that is unexpected. I have to ask now even if it may seem disrespectful.

"Why did you do it in the first place Ma?"

"She said you are dating." Her eyes are everywhere but me.

"Who?"

"Mam' Mngomezulu. She said you are dating and need protection as teen pregnancy is rife. That they admit a lot of young people at the clinic."

"And you believed her Ma, knowing how much she hates me."

"I panicked. I should have known better or suspected that she was up to no good." Sighing heavily and regretfully.

"She told the nurses that it was your idea---" Mom's eyes almost pop out of her head with shock.

"The nurses queried the use of Depo-Provera and she insisted that it was your idea which needed to be carried out." Mama is shaking with rage now and I give her a glass of water to calm her down.

"I am an illiterate woman who has never needed any of these things. I trusted her as the healthcare worker to know and do the right thing." There is pain and guilt as her eyes sweep over me. I feel and look pregnant. I don't recognise my body and am ashamed to even go out.

"What did I ever do to her mama?"

She takes me in her arms and cradles me in her chest as she rocks me back and forth. I finally release all the hurt and pent-up anger I have been carrying within for the past weeks. She wipes my face and makes us some tea when I am finally composed before making me seat opposite her.

"You know I should have suspected something was not right when she of all people took a sudden interest in our lives." Pausing briefly before proceeding. "Had I not panicked and trusted you I will have seen right through her."

There is a faraway expression before she picks up again.

"Your Aunt Betty came to live with us just before you were born. She took care of you until you were five and left soon after she gave birth to her baby boy." I have seen Aunt Betty at family events. She hardly ever visits and when she does it is usually for a day.

"The last time I saw them was on Christmas day at a family gathering and the son was there. He is the replica of Mr Mngomezulu. None of her girls look like him but the boy." What, well I have never paid much attention to my cousin. He is a boy, and I don't have time for boys whether blood related or not except for my dad.

"I think Mrs Mngomezulu always suspected that there was an affair between your aunt and her husband. The hostility though came after the boy was born. She came bearing gifts, took one look at the boy and left without uttering a word." *Yep, a woman's instinct cannot be ignored.*

"She could see even then who it belonged to. I think she blamed us for the affair."

How, mom and dad are never home. They are always working. How can they be expected to police two consenting adults? Madness.

"She waited all these years to exact revenge and then decided that messing up with my reproductive organs was the way to go, yhoo?" That's evil, it truly lives within her. Who does that to an innocent child? Why did she not have it out with my aunt, her husband or even my parents? Wow.

"I am so sorry my child for entrusting your health to her. She was so friendly and thoughtful when she approached me, acting like a concerned parent."

"Mrs Mngomezulu though mom?"

"Yeah, I know. I messed up big time." Shrugging regretfully.

"Ah well, nothing can be done for me now, but she will regret what she started."

"What do you mean?"

"Nah, I won't shoot her. Don't look so alarmed. I will deal with her naturally. She is not going to cause havoc with another's woman's child ever again." I squeeze her hands to show that all is forgiven and ask that from here on we keep the communication lines open. I need her to trust me and to engage with me on matters that concern me, especially those that have far-reaching effects.

Parents are up and already out of the house at six AM the next morning. I prepare myself and wait for Mrs Mngomezulu to step out.

"Morning Ma." I pounce respectfully as she prepares to leave.

She nods disdainfully whilst taking in my deformed body.

"Off to the clinic to bungle another's child's life." I quiz.

She stutters unsure where I am headed.

"Oh, we had a discussion with mama yesterday regarding the changes in my body and your hand in it."

"It is not my fault that you are raised by an illiterate mom who is raising a loose kid like her…"

"Whoa whoa stop it right there."

"Oh what! You little brat, what do you want?" Such arrogance needs to be smacked.

"To talk and get clarity but it is clear that is not going to work. I am going to hound you. Wherever you go and whatever you do I will be right there beside you. I will be the first thing that you see and last thing that you think of before you sleep." She sneers scornfully.

"I am going to make your life miserable. Mark my words." I turn towards home to fetch my books and lock up. She laughs in that irritating sarcastic manner of hers.

"Let the games begin." I state. That moron knows nothing about me. I live and thrive on creating experiments from the little lab I created in my room. Stephen King, Takashi Shimizu, Anne Rice and James Wan are some of my heroes, hhe uzozwa ngathi uyasha (she will feel like she is burning) when I am done with her. We have tolerated her nonsense for the longest time. It is not my parents' fault that her husband could not stay faithful and committed to their marriage.

Later that night we are woken by screams coming from Mrs Mngomezulu's home. All their lights are blazing, theirs is the only house with electricity in our street, and we can see shadows moving around. We observe and after a while go back to sleep. Nothing to do with us as we are not wanted there.

The horrors seem to follow Mrs Mngomezulu wherever she goes. Her paranoia reaches fever pitch at work until she is requested to take leave for her sanity and safety of patients as she has started hallucinating. It is claimed that she can't sleep and suffers from anxiety attacks. They say on some days she wakes up calling my name repeatedly and neighbours are surprised at this as they know that she hates me with passion and that I have made sure to steer clear of her. This continues for a while until one day, there is a knock on our door. There is Mrs Mngomezulu standing there looking haggard and thirty kilograms lighter.

"Sawubona makhi, may I please come in?" How humble, I think as I observe her coming in and sitting opposite me with her hands tightly clenched on top of the table.

"It is enough now ntombazana, it must stop." Mom looks at her and then at me with surprise.

"What are you talking about Mrs Mngomezulu?"

"She knows." Without bothering to look at ma.

"Ntombi, what is happening?"

"Nothing Ma, she suffers from illusions. I told her she won't rest after what she did to me and now her brain is playing tricks on her, it is on overdrive." Mrs Mngomezulu draws a deep breath and stands as if about to attack me. Ma jumps up ready to defend me. I ask her to take a seat. The woman has no energy to even walk let alone take us on.

"Are you able to stop the bleeding?" I don't mention that I researched about Yarrow tea and its wonders. The bleeding has finally stopped.

"No." She mumbles in response.

"Can you return my breasts to their perkiness?"

"No."

"The tummy?"

"That is easy, you can exercise or walk it off."

"Easy for you to say. You can afford gym fees and healthy food. I am not walking eight kilometres to school to shed tummy fat I did not have before you came along." I can tell that both adults are shocked by my boldness.

"I can pay for your gym subscription. Just stop with this nonsense now. It is enough!"

Mama gives me that look again which I completely ignore. I shake my head slowly and proffer that evil smile she usually reserves for me.

"I can't Ma. You woke the evil residing within me. I won't stop until you apologise."

"Ntombi, what do you mean?"

"Mind games mama, mind games. Only the strongest will survive. Goodbye Mrs Mngomezulu and do keep your eyes open at night as you never know what might wander inside your bedroom."

I give her another evil smile before leaving them sitting there in bewilderment as I head to my room. I am tired of all this drivel. She has not repented at all, there was no apology. Just expectations and entitlement that we will do as she asks. Nx.

I decide to up the ante. She is not going to rest now. She will see me at every turn where there is a mirror in sight. I will be in her house, work, taxi, church, stores. Wherever she goes my apparition will be right there until she breaks completely. I want that brain to turn into mush. I bunk school in the coming days to concentrate on experiments, until…

"Ntombi!"

"Ma?" I come out of my room quickly thinking she has hurt herself or something. Her tone sounded odd and urgent.

"It's Mrs Mngomezulu." Gasping with shock.

"What does she want now?"

"She threw herself in front of a moving train."

"Wow." Interesting, so she preferred death than humbling herself enough to come and apologise for her deeds.

"You don't sound surprised. What did you do?"

"Nothing Ma. I just played on her weaknesses but what happened is all on her." I leave her for my room to think. I am relieved that the devil has ended her life but not sure if that is the ending I was craving. I need to start attending church again to ask for forgiveness for my part in this. The mind is a powerful tool which can be manipulated at will when the target least expects it.

Yeah, I partly played a role in her madness, but it was all her in the end. May her evil spirit find relief in the afterlife. I'm done. I have to dispose of this apparatus in case the police decide to come snooping around. After all my name has been thrown about by Mrs Mngomezulu.

My work is complete though. No other child will ever endure what I have gone through at that woman's hand. I should feel elated but instead I am left numb. She was weak and couldn't handle her own medicine. Strange for such a mean-spirited heart. Parents really need to create a dialogue and healthy communication lines with their kids. None of this mess will have happened had mom held that bees and birds talk with me instead of involving that witch.

Slaves in a foreign land

Discontented voices raged with anger
"Go back home, we don't want you"
Smug responses vibrated back
"Silly, lazy, useless nation. We are here to stay"
Despair engulfed the locals
Young ones hid in the shadows of their rooms
So, it raged, nationals against locals
Until locals could fight no more
Then nationals turned against each other
"Help us, we are perishing"
Deafening silence, nothing left
They thought they were smarter
But they were slaves just as the locals were before
attaining freedom
Slaves in a foreign land with nowhere to go
Darkness was their only salvation from the slaughter

Author Bio

Busisiwe Ngwenya is the author of two short story books, *Triumph of a Deserving Person* and *Waiting For Me,* which are available on Amazon Kindle.

She is also a Co-founder at LeeBeeCrock Media, a film production and development company. Some of her stories have been published by Zoba's Facilities and Fundza Literacy.